Ashley could feel pain and sorrow in the small, plain room. It was a clear and fresh impression. From the moment that she stepped into the room she could feel it. She knew that Catherine sensed something as well.

Catherine glanced at Ashley while she folded her clothes and asked, "You feel it too?"

Ashley nodded. "Something definitely went down here. I feel some really strong impressions of pain and loss. I have been sitting here trying to get a handle on it, but so far it escapes me."

Catherine sat on the bed next to her and rubbed Ashley's shoulders. Her brows were knit in concentration. "Well, this is a halfway house of sorts. Perhaps somebody had a hard time here and that's what we're feeling."

Ashley shivered. The feeling she got from merely sitting in the room was stronger than that. It felt like death . . . Cold and never ending. It hung in the air and clung to the wallpaper. She wondered what the night would hold as the moon rose higher and filled the room with shadows.

OUT
OF THE
NIGHT

KRIS BRUYER

THE NAIAD PRESS, INC.
1996

Printed in the United States of America on acid-free paper
First Edition

Editor: Lisa Epson
Cover designer: Bonnie Liss (Phoenix Graphics)
Typesetter: Sandi Stancil

Library of Congress Cataloging-in-Publication Data
Bruyer, Kris. 1962–
    Out of the night / by Kris Bruyer.
        p.   cm.
    ISBN 1-56280-120-1 (pbk.)
    I. Title.
PS3562.R846098   1996
813'.54—dc20   95-39247
                                                                      CIP

For my mother,
who believed . . .
I miss you.

And
for Cary . . .
From out of the night,
there always comes
the dawn.
I love you, my friend.

About the Author

Kris Bruyer lives in Spokane Washington with her partner, four cats and a dog. Currently studying law, she plans to fight for the rights of women and children.

Sachet, Idaho
August 19, 1902

Eliza paused for a moment and leaned her tall frame against the cool wall of the mine. Wisps of hair had fallen from the tight bun she had set in her hair that morning, and now, she pushed them away from her face. Toward the back wall, she watched Alex working with a pick chipping away at the rock.

Lean and muscular, Alex could pass for a man easily, and she had done so many times when they both lived in New York those long years ago. Even now, Alex wore her hair short like most men and found men's clothes much more comfortable to her body. It was her choice, and Eliza loved her the way that she was.

"It will be time for supper soon," Eliza called from where she stood. Through the din of the pick hitting solid rock, she wondered if Alex had even heard her and then Alex turned.

"Yah, and I've worked up a bit of hunger, too," Alex said with the thick Irish brogue that was as distinct as when she first came to the New World as a child. Alex turned to give the stubborn wall a few more whacks before retiring back to the cabin.

Eliza stared down at the pickax. This was not what she had hoped for when she left New York with Alex almost two years ago. She reminded herself that she hadn't been sure what to expect. Two women and a child of eleven riding a train across the United States, then three days on horseback to this piece of God's untamed country to mine for gold. She believed that Alex could do anything; that was why she had come.

For a moment, she tried to remember the splendor that was New York. She had been a woman of means and influence at her husband's side. His prestige was her prestige, and she had attended some of the most glamorous balls of the age. She had even danced with President McKinley when he visited New York.

The women spoke in circles of her chastity and passion while secretly envying her beauty and position. Men undauntedly challenged her fidelity but found that bridge not passable. Eliza could not

2

fathom being with anyone but her husband, and she found that to be, at the best of times, a chore. And so she remained on the social scene to be the beautiful ice queen of New York City.

The first time she had seen Alexandria O'Connor was at the theater. Alexandria, or Alex as she was known then, was fast becoming one of the most popular actors of the stage. With her short red hair and smoothly cut features, she made a handsome man. Women of prosperity, never knowing that within beat the heart of a woman, swooned in their chairs as the actor took the stage. Acting was the only way Alex could find to support her brother after her parents died. Being a woman, she knew her choices were few. She could prostitute her body to keep the boy warm and fed, she could be a servant for the rich people she hated, or she could act.

Alex found acting to be the best choice of all, so with her father's clothes on and her long hair cut short, she sought a job as an actor. Luckily, she found a company that needed a young man with an Irish brogue and was hired.

Eliza watched the play that night next to her husband and found her heart beating wildly in her chest. She could not remember the name of the play nor what it was about, but she remembered the actor.

Several weeks later, Eliza and her husband attended a large garden party at the house of her husband's friend. She was not surprised to find the young actor there. It was not uncommon for people of importance to entertain those who belonged to the arts, though to Eliza it seemed cruel. It was almost like caging a beautiful animal and watching it from the other side of the bars, both knowing that it could never belong to the world outside the cage.

Eliza joined a group of women near the rose gardens who spoke in hushed tones while her husband and some gentlemen were discussing points of politics. Though she scolded herself for it, Eliza found her eyes drawn to Alex O'Connor repeatedly.

He moved among men and women as though he was not comfortable with either group. Eliza put his discomfort down to his age and social background. She was not aware of the secret he was hiding.

"I do believe that he is the best looking thing to come along since the dawn of time," a woman with a soft accent said very close to Eliza. Quickly, Eliza turned her attention away from Alex, but not before some other women caught the look on her face. "What do you think, Mrs. Wittacker," the southern accented woman asked, grasping Eliza by her arm. Eliza smiled curtly; the ice queen was not going to melt dead away and certainly not in this crowd of people who she knew waited for the day.

"I have seen better, my dear," Eliza said, twirling her parasol casually on her shoulder. A hushed murmur went through the crowd of women as they gossiped a few feet away.

With the reluctant Alex O'Connor on his heels, a young man with a wide-grinning face approached the knot of women who stood shaded by the sun with their brilliant array of colored parasols and summer silks. "My dear, I would like to introduce you to one of the most brilliant young men I have met in my life," the young man said, grinning as he approached. Eliza felt the young woman grip her arm tightly before she let go and stepped forward to greet her husband.

"I am ever so pleased to make your acquaintance, Mr. O'Connor," the woman said curtsying slightly. "It is my pleasure," Alex said exchanging pleasantries. Eliza could feel eyes on her as she was introduced as well. When her eyes met the soft blue eyes of the Irish actor, she knew it had happened. She could feel her heart begin to flutter and a warmth flush over her. Alex's eyes seemed to be clouded with other thoughts, and Eliza could not read them.

After a moment, Alex excused himself and moved on through the crowd. Eliza watched every movement he made. She wasn't sure what made her dig into the small bag that she carried and pull out her calling card, but she knew that she could not bear to never see those eyes again. As delicately as she could, she moved toward one of the men who was waiting on the people at the party and handed him the card. "Would you please assure that Mr. O'Connor gets this before he leaves?" she asked, moving away before he could answer.

It was months later that Eliza saw her calling card again. Since she had never handed out her card to anyone before Alex, she knew who was being announced at the door.

Her husband was out for the day, and she was walking along the extensive grounds of her husband's house. The beauty of the roses and other flowers and blooming shrubs enchanted her. She daydreamed of things never imagined by other women of her time.

Eliza nodded, "Show him the gardens, please." As the doorman turned to show her guest in, Eliza felt her heart racing. She had never thought that he would come, this proud Irishman, and yet he was here. Whatever would they talk about? What could she find in common with this aloof man from another country? she asked, quizzing herself. Before she could answer, she heard a soft voice behind her. It lacked the gruffness that she had grown accustomed to in her husband's voice.

She turned to find the handsome young man holding his hat in his hands. He seemed frightened and unsure. For the first time in years, Eliza smiled and found herself laughing inside. "Come, sit with me," she said, finding shade underneath a willow tree on a bench there. After a moment's hesitation, Alex followed and sat at a comfortable distance from her.

"I don't think it's proper for me to be here without an escort of sorts, you bein' a woman and all." Alex twirled his hat in his hands nervously.

Eliza smiled. "Thank you for worrying about my reputation, sir, but I don't think that anyone will know that you have been here. I trust my servants not to speak of this."

"Why did ya ask me to come here?" Alex asked bluntly.

For a long time, Eliza gazed out across the grass and gardens. Her thoughts were well hidden behind a solid mask of resistance on her beautiful face. She could lie and hope that he would understand the meaning behind the words, or she could tell the truth. "I'm not sure why I gave you my card. I find myself helplessly attracted to you, and I wish to spend time in your company."

Alex tensed. "That doesn't surprise me, you know. Just last week, I paid a visit to your friend, Mrs.

Tippton. After she talked extensively about her home in the South, she asked me to become her lover. And before that it was Mrs. Quincy. I must say that you have started quite a trend. After I received your card, at least a dozen other ladies discretely sent me theirs. I guess that they merely followed suit after you. I am not for sale to anyone for any price, Mrs. Wittacker. I am a poor actor trying to support my younger brother, that's all."

Alex stood and tapped his hat on his leg for a moment before he turned. Eliza could hear the pain in his voice that betrayed the anger in his eyes. "Please, tell your friends not to send me their cards, nor their affections. I'll not accept them anymore."

With that Alex left, leaving Eliza behind. She had never known desire so much nor the disappointment of refusal.

All of the women who associated in the same group as Eliza kept their own counsel about Alex. No one asked Eliza if her meeting with the actor had gone any better. Instead, they clung to the arms of their husbands and dreamed of the actor that performed on the stage below them. Eliza and her husband enjoyed the theater, and Eliza found herself there at least once a week in her own private box with him. From a distance, she watched as Alex changed faces, names, and characters like one would change shirts.

Eliza sent her calling card to him repeatedly but was never graced with his presence. In an act of foolish desperation, she commissioned a man to make a special straight-edged razor with an ivory handle on it. She requested that he engrave *To my love, From Eliza* on the blade. She told the man that it was a present for her husband. When it was completed, she sent by servant the razor, a specially designed china shaving cup with Alex's initials on it, and a badger-hair shaving brush to Alex's door. When the servant returned, Eliza grilled the man for hours until she knew every detail from the conversation that ensued to the clothes that Alex wore. For days her heart pounded every time a servant entered the room to announce a visitor. To her dismay, Alex sent a note of gratitude for the gift. *It was much too intimate, I shouldn't have done it,* Eliza often chided herself. But deep inside, she plotted and planned for the next time that she could find herself alone with him. Her opportunity came a month later, near Christmas of 1887.

With her husband out of town on business, Eliza found herself in the company of her parents who had come in from Philadelphia for the festive season. Her father had heard of a wonderful young actor who had been performing in New York and had insisted that Eliza take them to a play.

From her balcony seat above the swarming crowds below, Eliza watched Alex play an old and tired man who was dying with such precision that she found tears flowing from her eyes at the end of the drama.

As the house lights began to glow, her father stated, "Brilliant. What a brilliant young man. I haven't seen anyone perform that part better in my life." Eliza smiled. From inside his pocket, her father pulled one of his cards and gave it to the usher standing stiffly inside the curtained box. "Would you be so kind, young man, as to give this to Alex O'Connor and tell him that I wish to dine with him tonight. I have written the address on the back."

Eliza could feel her stomach flopping inside. He would have to come now — her father was a justice with the state supreme court of Pennsylvania.

The dinner party that evening was elegant, and the Wittacker household entertained a dozen of the most influential people in New York. Eliza watched Alex. She could tell that he felt out of place as he stood in a corner of the room where everyone had retired after eating. The room boomed with conversation and laughter. Men drank whiskey and smoked fat cigars as the women sat in pairs and trios on daintily cushioned seats and gossiped.

Eliza moved carefully across the room to where Alex stood alone. No one seemed to notice as she spoke with him for a moment, nor had anyone seemed to pay attention when she disappeared into another room.

Mrs. Tippton followed Alex with her eyes as he slipped out of the room behind Eliza. After a few moments, she excused herself and followed.

A light snow fell as Eliza stepped out into the night. She knew that everything she had here would be gone if she were caught, but she was certain that no one had seen her leave. In the silence she waited for Alex, who was not too far behind her.

"Come on, quickly, this way," Eliza instructed as she pulled Alex away from the house down a path that led to the gazebo. Alex followed closely behind her.

Once in the safety of the darkness, Eliza turned on her heel toward Alex. "Did you not like my gift?" she asked pouting.

Alex raised a gloved hand. "You don't know what you are doing, girl."

Eliza crossed her brows. "I've always been one to pursue until the bitter end what I want. And don't call me girl. I am a woman, as you have plainly seen. Yes, I've felt your eyes on me. From across the room, you watch me and I watch you." A smile touched Eliza's face. It was a coy smile that hid behind it secret desires and images that she only dared to think about when all of the lamps were snuffed for the night and the darkness protected her thoughts from her husband.

Alex sighed and moved across the gazebo, his face reflecting a million thoughts. Eliza moved until she was within inches of touching Alex.

In the moonlight, she could see his eyes. She could see the fire of desire burning within him before he could squelch it by looking away. Daringly, Eliza touched his face and drew his lips to her own. The kiss lasted for less than a moment, but in that embrace Eliza found something that shook her to her very soul.

As Eliza pulled away she saw something like pain and repressed desire touch Alex's face. She felt, suddenly, very vulnerable. She took a few steps back. Alex twirled his hat in his hand as though he were dumbfounded by the kiss and could find no words to tell her that what she had read in his eyes was wrong. Tears sprang to her eyes as she turned and moved as briskly as she could away from the gazebo and into the night. She didn't see the woman who stood in the black protection of the bushes and plotted the best way to use what she had just seen to her advantage.

* * * * *

Eliza was jolted from her thoughts by a voice coming from the mouth of the mine. "Alexandria O'Connor," the voice called from the darkness. Eliza tried to focus her eyes beyond the torchlight to the shadows behind.

Alex turned from the vein she had just struck and stared at the jumping lights. She could not place the voice in her head. "Who are you?" Alex demanded as she moved toward the light. Slowly, the lights faded and the shadows beyond disappeared.

"What the hell was that all about?" Alex demanded. She could feel a knot of fear in her stomach. Eliza shook her head as she stared up at the mouth of the mine.

"By God, Jesus, do you think they have found us?" Alex asked, feeling for the pistol that she always carried at her side.

She felt Eliza tremble next to her. "I don't know."

Suddenly, from the place where Alex had been picking at the wall, the earth began to give in. "Run, Eliza, the whole damned thing's giving in. Run," Alex screamed as the shaft began to fill with dust and flying rocks.

Eliza ran and fell. She felt Alex lift her up and push her on. From behind, a fist-size rock struck Alex on the back of her neck and knocked her down.

At the mouth of the mine, Eliza turned. She saw the still body of her lover lying on the ground. Debris and wooden supports were giving way and falling near Alex. "Alex," Eliza screamed as she tried to get to her.

From out of the cabin, a teenaged boy with a two-year-old child in tow came running. He stood helplessly at the mouth of the mine while his sister and the child's mother were buried in the collapsing earth. In an instant, he knew that everything was lost. The child screamed and cried, more from the commotion than from the realization of her mother's demise.

He lifted the child into his arms and cuddled her until she stopped crying. Several times he found himself close to tears as he stood where the mine entrance had been.

A second later, his grief was interrupted when he heard riders coming over the trail that led to the cabin. The boy knew that no one ever came that way except the men that his sister and Eliza feared. They never had company, and no one knew their business.

Quickly, the boy took the child into the barn and opened a part of the wooden floor inside one of the stalls. Underneath, Alex had dug out a hole big enough for all of them to hide in if they ever had to. The boy and child descended into the black hole and rearranged the boards over it.

In the darkness, he heard the voices as booted feet moved swiftly through the night. He heard the cabin door opening and shouts coming from inside and outside of the house. The boy was not afraid until he heard feet moving through the barn. With his hand over the mouth of the child in his arms, he watched through the cracks in the floor as the men moved over the top of his head in the stall.

After a moment, the light faded as the booted feet moved to other parts of the barn. He heard a shout from the outside, and heavy footsteps responded from within the barn.

The boy knew that the men had found the rubble

entrance of the mine. He could hear them talking in broken sentences outside.

"They're not here, John," one man said.

"Looks like this cave-in here was recent," another said.

There was a great pause, and the boy had almost convinced himself that the men had gone when he heard a man shout in anger and in pain. "Eliza!"

ONE

Olivia stood at the window of her room and watched the sun go down over the mountainside. A chill ran through her though the evening was still very warm. She used to enjoy the sunset. Now, it was an omen for darker things. Soon they would come, just as they had every night for the past thirty years that the school had stood on this ground. She had never really noticed them before, since they were mere shadows that moved out there. Lately, however, they had become louder and more intolerable. The girls who stayed at the school had begun to leave one by one until only a handful remained behind. She feared that everything she and her husband had worked so long for would be gone. Stoically, she stood at the window and watched.

The glimmer of torches rose over the hill. As the men came closer, she could hear the beat of horse hooves on the ground. They dismounted and scurried around the grounds. A few men walked toward the cabin; they quickly ransacked the tiny two-room abode.

"Looks like they were just here," one man said to another as they rushed from the cabin. The pair surveyed the grounds until they found the collapsed mine.

"John, you'd better come and see this," one of the men called. From the barn a shadowy figure of a man came with a torch. He was a man of considerable wealth, and the air about him seemed to move in a different way than it did around the other men.

Worry and fear were written on his face. His face also showed darker things, like rage.

The apparition ended the same every time. The man would examine the collapsed mine. He would listen to the men as they spoke in hushed tones. And then he would turn his face to the night sky and scream out, "Eliza." After that, all would vanish in front of her like elusive wisps of smoke.

Olivia shivered. She had tried everything possible to rid her school of the apparitions that wandered the hallways and the grounds. She had even tried to get a Catholic priest to come out and exorcise the school, but he politely informed her that the church doesn't do that sort of thing anymore.

Olivia shook her head. Tonight's apparition was only part of her problems. On other nights, when the moon was full, the rest would come. And those times were the worst of all.

She knew when they were coming because the hair on her arms would stand up. Clothed in the blackest robes so they seemed to not disturb the night, they would come. Their incantations rose in the air like billows of smoke. They spoke words that she could not understand, in a monotone that seemed to lull even the winds into sleep.

The first couple of times Olivia told her daughter, only to be informed that she was probably having "a hell of a nightmare." She always could sense when they were coming again, and the next time she made her daughter stand at the window to watch with her. They came in pairs, with their black robes, over the rise of the hill. The night stilled until the only sound that could be heard was their spell spoken in unison.

"Holy Jesus," her daughter breathed beside her. "What in the hell are they doing out there?"

Olivia shrugged as she watched the group gather around the forgotten mine. "Stay here, Mother." Olivia felt her daughter touch her hand before she left. She heard the phone being dialed in the living room of the apartment that they shared.

After a moment of conversation, she heard the sound of the receiver as it was slammed into its cradle. She joined her daughter. "What is it, Amanda? What's wrong?" Olivia asked as she followed her daughter to her bedroom.

Amanda unlocked the gun case in her closet and pulled out a 20-gauge from its resting place. "They say it is going to take them at least twenty minutes if not more to get out here." She loaded the shotgun and slid back the pump action.

In panic, Olivia followed behind her. "Amanda, you can't go out there and just start shooting people."

The woman took the stairs two at a time. "Why not, Mother? They are trespassing on private property."

Olivia could not keep the alarm out of her voice. "Baby, don't go out there. What if they are armed? Or what if they curse you or something?"

Amanda stopped in her tracks. She would have laughed if the situation wasn't so serious. "I'll be careful. I'm just going to scare them off. Okay? Stay here."

Olivia nodded but followed her daughter to the door. When Amanda slid back the dead bolt and pulled the door open, not one head turned in their direction. Amanda felt a shiver run the length of her spine as she stepped out onto the porch.

Twelve people dressed in black stood in a semicircle around the mouth of the old mine. Amanda could understand only one word that came from the indiscernible gibberish of the people, *Alexandria*. They called for a woman named Alexandria.

"Hey," Amanda called. Her voice trembled slightly as she approached the group. In unison, the group turned to face her. There were no faces that Amanda could see. A chill tickled her spine.

One of the people pulled a small knife from a baggy sleeve. Amanda brought the shotgun up in an instant. "Clear out. I've called the police."

Whispered words began to fall out of the faceless robes as the bold one approached with the knife. Amanda could feel her finger pulling back the trigger. She would fire if the figure crossed the imaginary line that she had drawn in her head.

"I am warning you," Amanda breathed through clenched teeth.

The figure paused for a moment. "No, I'm warning you, Amanda. Leave while you can still draw your own breath." The voice was soft and feminine.

Amanda heard her mind scream as the figure crossed the imaginary line. Closely behind her the others followed. The next sound was the blast from the shotgun. Her ears rang as she threw the pump action and a spent cartridge spun through the air. In an instant another round was in the barrel, but there was nothing to aim at.

A lone figure lay on the ground in a pool of moonlight. A large red spot stained the front of the robe. Amanda carefully approached the figure.

Olivia screamed something from the porch several times, but Amanda only heard the sound of her own blood pumping in her ears. After a minute, she figured that the woman was dead. She had shot her in the chest at close range.

She turned on her heels and ran to the porch. Olivia waited for her, screaming incoherently. She pulled her mother by the arm into the school and locked the door.

When the police arrived almost fifteen minutes later, Amanda led the officer to where she had shot the robed woman. Nothing was there. The body, along with all traces of blood, had disappeared.

Amanda stood in utter astonishment. The grass was not even bent where the body had lain.

The officer smiled kindly as she escorted Amanda back into the school and up into the women's apartment. Amanda knew that she did not believe her, and why should she? There was no trace of any sort of violence. It was almost as though she and her mother had imagined the whole thing.

Olivia wrote a letter to a woman named Madame Mistorie in Portland. Olivia had tried all other avenues, and this was the last one. She had heard about Madame Mistorie from a friend who had visited her once a month to have her fortune told. The friend had said that this psychic could be trusted. She only hoped that Madame Mistorie could arrive soon and help her and Amanda before it was too late.

TWO

Emily breezed in through the back entrance of the bookstore with Teri following behind with most of the luggage. She could hear muffled conversations coming from the front of the store as she wound her way past bookshelves that held dusty tomes covering subjects from astral projection to witchcraft in the nineties.

Emily was excited. This was her second real mission beyond her own hole-in-the-wall business where she, as Madame Mistorie, read tarot and palms and occasionally used her unique gifts to tell the future. She could not keep the words *we're going on a witch-hunt* from coming into her head. But that was only because Ashley, her best friend, kept putting it like that. Emily tried at least a hundred times to tell her friend that it was simply an investigation, not a witch-hunt.

"Why do you need me to go?" Emily heard Ashley ask as she rounded the last shelf of books.

"I don't want to go without you, that's why. And besides, Emily would be hurt if we didn't go," Catherine's voice pleaded.

Emily dropped the small case that she was carrying on the glass counter where some crystals and other things like copper and iron charms were kept. She could not believe that Ashley was still thinking about not going. Just the night before Emily had spent hours on the phone persuading Ashley to reconsider. She thought that she had been successful.

"So you still don't want to go, huh?" Emily asked with her hands on her hips.

Ashley flushed slightly. She could not explain the fear that she felt knotting in her stomach every time she thought about one of Emily's adventures. The last time Ashley had followed Emily, she had almost died and had met with some very real fears. It was not her idea of fun.

Emily crossed the room and clutched her friend by the shoulders and looked into her eyes. "I promise you, Ashley, that nothing bad will happen to you this time. I know these things." And, Emily did. She had the gift of seeing things before they happened sometimes. She knew that Ashley was in no danger and that the trip might do her some good. In her heart, Emily knew that in order for the whole

21

investigation to go well, she would need to have available the powers that all her friends possessed.

Patricia appeared from one of the side doors with her reading glasses perched on her nose. She was wiping the dust from a very old book when she looked up and saw Emily. Her brightly painted lips spread with a warm smile. "Emily, you made it." The two women embraced.

"Ma, Emily just came from across town, for God's sake," Ashley said, rolling her eyes. She knew that whenever the two of them got around each other it was like a homecoming for the prodigal son.

Patricia waved off her daughter's comment and turned her attention to the large book she had found in the back storage area. "I thought this might come in handy." She handed the book carefully to Emily, who studied the front cover. A broad grin crossed her face as she nodded.

"I knew that somewhere in all of your many books you would be able to find what we needed." Emily tucked the large, heavy book into one of her suitcases.

"Well, looks like we're all here." For the first time Patricia turned her attention to Teri. "How are you doing, Teri? You're ever so quiet back there."

Teri smiled, "I'm doing okay."

Emily pouched her lip out to sulk when she said, "Ashley's not going." She knew that out of all the people in the world, Patricia could persuade her daughter to go even if she had to hog-tie her and force her.

Patricia pulled her glasses off of her nose and tucked them away in the case before she turned her attention to Ashley. "Ashley Mae, you're going to send your mother, your best friend, and your lover into the possible brink of utter terror and hellfire, into the very eye of the storm, into the devil's playground without even attempting to make sure we all get back here in one piece? That does not sound like my daughter. The one who works with me every day of the week. The one who worries about me without letting it show. The one who —"

Ashley raised her hand, "All right, all right, I'll go, but only because Catherine won't go without me and you need her."

Emily grinned. "Who's driving?" she asked as she pulled the small luggage bag onto her shoulder.

"I am," Patricia said, pulling her keys out of her handbag.

"No, Ma, I've seen your driving. I'll drive." Ashley pulled the keys from her mother's hands before Patricia could say anything and disappeared to the rear of the store.

THREE

"Are we there yet?" Emily asked as she squirmed in the backseat of the Lincoln. She had long since grown bored of watching the scenery as it passed by her. Even as a child she couldn't abide sitting in a car for any length of time.

Patricia looked in the backseat over her reading glasses. "We're about ten miles outside of Wallace, and from there we need to go another twenty miles. So in the long run I would say yes, we are almost there."

Emily breathed a sigh of relief. "Thank God. I thought I was just going to die of boredom."

Catherine smiled, "This might be a good time for us to get our thoughts together on how we are going to investigate this case."

Emily nodded. From inside her carrying case, she pulled out a letter that she had read and reread so many times that the paper was starting to get worn. She had even tried to find some psychic impressions or residue on it so that she could know exactly what they were dealing with.

"I get the impression that there is some real danger for the women. I don't think that the hauntings are really what they need to worry about right now. We can deal with those poor lost souls later. The real problem comes from a more physical source." Emily passed the letter to Catherine, who also had read the note several times. Her eyes quickly scanned the page. She found nothing new and handed it forward to Patricia.

"The woman mentions in the letter a school of some sort. Do you know what type of school would be out there in the middle of nowhere?" Catherine asked, touching her slender finger to her lips.

Emily shrugged. "I suppose it is some sort of private school for girls. I had a hard time envisioning it when I tried to get impressions off the paper. The most that I could see was that it was set back in the mountains and that the school was placed in the middle of a piece of land that had been cleared of trees. Somewhere on the property are a corral and a big barn with horses. I got a subtle impression of a mine shaft somewhere on the property. And, Ashley, you're going to love this — there's a cabin on the land."

Ashley wrinkled her nose. "Why would that turn me on?"

Emily shrugged, "I just know you, my friend. You like old things. Maybe you'll find an old penny in there or something."

Patricia changed the subject. "It's too bad that Teri couldn't come. I'll miss her."

Emily nodded and looked a bit forlorn. She already missed Teri terribly. She would miss her even more in the week that lay ahead. The only solace that she felt was that Teri had promised that she would try to join them on the weekend when Gretchen was out of school.

"Welcome to Wallace, Idaho," Ashley read from a colorful sign as she slowed the car. The women took in the splendor of the scenery. Ashley allowed her eyes to leave the road briefly to take in the deep greens of the mountainside. Everything seemed to move at a snail's pace, even the people. Ashley waited for an elderly woman followed by a handful of children to cross the street. "Okay. Where to now, Madame Mistorie?"

Emily studied the makeshift map. "Turn right up here. Then take a left on Placer Creek. We go about twenty more miles and the school should be right before we get to Sachet." Ashley nodded and steered the car onto a narrow road.

"Thank God you've got good shocks on this baby," Emily commented as Ashley turned on a dirt road. To one side a brown forestry sign read: AVERY 30, SACHET 21, SLATE CREEK 8.

"Come on, ladies, the road isn't that bad," Ashley

commented as she dodged a few potholes that marked the county road. That was a feat in itself as it had rained recently and the muddy water hid the depressions from sight.

Emily looked out of the windshield from the rear seat. "Right before we get to Sachet, you need to take a left. According to this map, it is the only road off this one before you get to the town."

Ashley nodded. "I wonder how the fishing is up here," she asked no one in particular. It had been many years since she had had the opportunity to cast a line in a stream. In fact, she had not been fishing since before her father had died. He was the one who had taught her creek and fly fishing. Suddenly she felt a bit lonely. She wondered if she would ever enjoy the sport quite the same if she tried it again.

"Ashley, turn here," Emily said suddenly. Ashley touched the brakes a bit too hard. The car came to a dead stop, and all the women were thrust forward in their seats. Patricia could not let the moment pass by without a comment. "Talk about my driving, willya."

"Sorry," Ashley apologized as she put the car in reverse and backed up. A large, wooden, hand-sculpted sign to their right told them they were on the right road.

Emily could feel her stomach doing flip-flops. While she loved her mission in life and her gift of second sight, she was not so foolish as to under-estimate the powers that other people possessed and used to twist people, events, and things to their own means.

Quite abruptly, the forest gave way to a perfectly sculptured lawn dotted with rose bushes and other flowers. A hedge followed the roadside as it led to the circular driveway in front of the school. Made of red brick, the three-story school looked much older than it really was. Emily guessed that in its day the school housed as many as a hundred students comfortably.

A couple of teenaged girls watched as the strange car pulled into the driveway. They didn't recognize the car, nor did they bother to greet it. From their bench seats, they watched openly as four women stepped out into the sunlight.

One of the girls snickered when she saw two of the women. They tried to decide who looked more unusual, the woman with the bright red hair that stood every which way on her head or the younger gal who wore the long, black skirt with the bright designs.

"Well, I like her hat, anyway," one of the girls commented.

The other nodded in agreement. "I wonder why they're here?" the girl said, knitting her brows.

"Who cares," the thinner girl said, standing and stretching. "Maybe they're here to chase off Mrs. Michaels's ghosts."

The shorter girl rose and furrowed her eyebrows, "I hope not. I kinda like them."

With this her friend chided, "Sometimes I think that you're just as nutty as Mrs. Michaels. Come on. Let's go see if Amanda will let us ride before supper."

Emily stretched and tried to rub the tiredness out of her legs. She watched the girls across the way as they stared openly at her. They were dressed in dark blue skirts and sweaters with white blouses. She wondered what they were talking about. Her thoughts were interrupted by a stocky, redheaded woman who approached from the corral.

"Can I help you, ladies," the woman asked as she removed a pair of leather gloves. Emily smiled, though the woman didn't seem to be too friendly. "Are you Mrs. Olivia Michaels?"

The woman shook her head, "No, that's my mother. What can I do for you?"

Emily pulled out the letter she had received and handed it to the woman. "I'm Madame Mistorie." The woman did not look amused at all.

As the woman read the letter, her lips turned down. "Look, ladies, I am afraid that you have wasted your time coming all the way here from Oregon, but I can assure you that there has been some kind of mistake. We don't need your kind out here causing trouble." The woman returned the letter to Emily.

Emily remained undaunted. "I should think that Mrs. Olivia Michaels can make that determination herself since she seems to have been the one who drafted this letter."

Ashley felt her gut sinking as she watched the pair challenge each other with words. She knew that Emily was not about to give ground, and judging the other woman she was not prepared to give any either.

"My mother is in no condition to be bothered. This whole thing has made her ill. Now please, just get in your car and drive back to Portland." The woman shoved the gloves into her back pocket. She squinted her eyes and tried to scare the other woman.

Emily crossed her arms. "We have driven a long

way to help you. I know what I'm doing, and I'm very good at it. Just give us a chance."

"This is private property. You are trespassing. I will expect all of you to be in your car and gone by the time I come back out," the woman said as she turned on her heel and walked toward the front entrance of the school.

Before she could reach her destination, one side of the double doors opened and a frail looking woman stepped out. The two women argued for a moment before the younger one, in a fury, disappeared down a pathway that led toward the corral and the barn behind.

Emily met the older woman halfway. She was taken by the muddy brown aura that shone around the woman. Emily knew instantly that the trouble that plagued the school had spent a great deal of its time sucking the life energy out of the woman.

"Madame Mistoire," the older woman smiled. The woman's back remained straight, though Emily knew the woman was in pain.

"Emily. Please, call me Emily."

The older woman nodded, and the smile never left her face. "I am Olivia Michaels." She scanned the rest of the women quickly.

Emily followed her gaze. "They're my friends who have come with me to help you. They can all be trusted."

The woman laid her hand on Emily's arm and smiled. "No offense, honey, but anymore I have trouble trusting anyone. I guess that I have spent too much time with my daughter, Amanda. I guess it's not her fault, she's just trying to protect me, but I must apologize for her behavior."

Emily waved her hand to clear the air of any bad vibes. "Don't worry about it. I'm sure that all of you are just a bit scared after the commotion that happened here before you wrote me."

"What commotion was that, dear?" Olivia asked. "I wrote you a very simple letter about some spirits that don't seem to know that they're dead. And I believe that I told you about some witches who insist on playing around the mine. But I never told you there was ruckus of any kind."

Emily could hear the fear in the woman's voice. She wondered how she could make the woman trust her and feel safe with her and her friends. "I am very good at what I do, Mrs. Michaels. If you had sent me a blank sheet of paper, I could have read your thoughts from it. I felt your fear and your concern. I also read some impressions like snapshots of the incident with the people in the black robes. You don't need to be concerned. If there's a way my friends and I will find it, and we'll drive out whatever evils haunt your school. I swear to you we will."

Olivia looked deep into Emily's eyes, trying to read the thoughts that flowed in the back of her mind. Emily opened her mind and allowed the woman to peer in. After a moment, the hand that gripped Emily's arm relaxed slightly. Emily breathed a sigh of relief and hoped that she really did know what she was talking about.

FOUR

Olivia Michaels sighed and sipped from her coffee before she spoke. "My husband and I dreamed of building a place for troubled girls. A school of sorts, I guess. We moved here in 1970 from New Jersey. My husband was a police sergeant, and I was a schoolteacher. We had some, ah, trouble before we decided to move here."

Emily watched the woman as she sat in a comfortable, overstuffed couch next to Ashley. She held her tongue and waited for the woman to continue, though she sensed already what the woman was going to say.

Olivia turned her gaze to Patricia. Her eyes pleaded for understanding. Patricia sat on the edge of her seat with her arms open in front of her. Both women were about the same age, and Olivia seemed to need the understanding of her peer.

"Amanda was wild back then. She seemed to have been born that way. Wild and carefree. Devil-may-care attitude. She started getting into trouble with the law when she was eleven, and by the time she was fifteen she was into drugs and drinking. She stayed out until all hours of the night and sometimes would not come home for days at a time.

"Then one night, when Amanda was seventeen, I got a phone call from Sam, my husband. He was calling from the precinct. Amanda and her friends were involved in some sort of a shooting incident. She swore she knew nothing about it, but the courts didn't believe her. She spent a hundred and twenty days in jail. The same day that she came home was the same day that we left for Idaho. Sam's great uncle had left him this land when he died, and we decided to open a place for girls who were troubled and needed a place to go."

"Your daughter seems to have turned out pretty good, considering," Patricia commented.

Olivia smiled. "The clean air and the quiet seem to turn people around. Maybe there is something in the fog of the bigger cities that poisons young minds."

"How many girls are staying here now?" Catherine asked, sipping from her coffee mug.

"Ten. Tomorrow it could be five. Ever since things started to happen around here with the spirits and that other thing, the girls have been leaving. The parents don't like to have their daughters up here with a crazy old woman. Even the government pulled its support when things started to unravel. That was when we lost most of the girls." Olivia sighed deeply. The lines on her face seemed to grow deeper as she thought about her troubles.

Ashley emphasized with her, and touched the woman's hand, arming it in her own. "We'll do the best that we can for you," Ashley said, trying to reassure the woman. She was glad that she had decided to come. For the first time she felt as though she could put her gifts to work for something good.

Amanda busied herself brushing down the horses when the girls came back from their ride. She had spent the last half of the day fuming over her mother's actions. She had taken care of the incident rather well. Whatever had happened that night when the witches came, Amanda knew that she had scared them. She had not seen anyone come near the mine since. Of course, she really wasn't looking for them. She preferred not to think about it.

The only thing that concerned her now was her mother. She had grown increasingly weak after the incident. Though she never complained, Amanda knew that she was in pain most of the time. Once Amanda had begged Olivia to go see a doctor, but Olivia brushed her off and said that she knew what was happening to her and that she had taken care of it.

A sour look crossed Amanda's face as she led one of the horses to its stall. This was how she took care of it, Amanda thought bitterly. And now they would probably lose the rest of the girls when their parents caught wind of what was going on. "Damn it," Amanda cursed.

"Hey, girl," someone said from the entrance of the barn. Amanda turned her attention to the voice and smiled while secretly glowing inside. It was the officer who had come out the night of the incident. Ever since that night, she had made regular stops. "Just to check up on things," she had said.

"Hey," Amanda said as she latched the stall gate shut. "What brings you out here, Officer Weston?" she asked, though she really didn't care as long as she came out.

Weston shoved her hands in the pockets of her jeans and shrugged. "Thought I'd come out and see how you and your mom are making out. I thought that maybe I'd see if you wanted to go fishing with me tomorrow morning."

Amanda tried to act casual as she leaned against an empty stall and rested her foot behind her on one of the wood slats. It had been a number of years since she had felt anything for anyone other than her parents. What stirred in her now threatened to engulf her. "Sure. What time were you thinking about going?"

Weston moved closer and leaned back against the same stall as Amanda. She crossed her arms in front of her. "I was thinking about maybe seven or so. There is some great creek fishing up above Sachet about twenty miles. I thought we could make a day of it."

"Sounds like fun," Amanda said as her heart beat wildly against her chest. She wished she had the nerve to touch this woman, to kiss this woman, to be with this woman. She found herself lost in a whirlwind of desire that cried out to be released.

"Great," Danielle Weston said as she tugged the keys to her truck from her pants pocket. Amanda followed her past the corral to the driveway.

"Looks like you've got visitors," Danielle said, nodding her head to the Lincoln parked in the circular driveway.

Amanda nodded, "Friends of my mother's." She smiled halfheartedly.

Danielle nodded. She heard the slight note of distaste in Amanda's voice. She sensed that something was going on and made a mental note to find out what. So far as she was concerned, the case that called her here almost a month ago was far from over, no matter what the police chief said.

FIVE

Ashley sat on the edge of one of the twin beds. She watched Catherine undress, though her thoughts were somewhere else.

Throughout the world, old emotions and some events left indelible marks. Ashley felt those scars here and probed them. She could feel pain and sorrow in the small, plain room. It was a clear and fresh impression. From the moment that she stepped into the room she could feel it. She knew that Catherine sensed something as well.

Catherine glanced at Ashley while she folded her clothes and asked, "You feel it too?"

Ashley nodded. "Something definitely went down here. I feel some really strong impressions of pain and loss. I have been sitting here trying to get a handle on it, but so far it escapes me."

Catherine sat on the bed next to her and rubbed Ashley's shoulders. Her brows were knit in concentration. "Well, this is a halfway house of sorts. Perhaps somebody had a hard time here and that's what we're feeling."

Ashley shivered. The feeling she got from merely sitting in the room was stronger than that. It felt like death in the cruelest sense. Cold and never ending. It hung in the air and clung to the wallpaper, and as the night progressed, the impressions became clearer and faster. She wondered what the night would hold as the moon rose higher and filled the room with shadows.

Olivia had given Emily the room between Ashley and Catherine's, and Patricia's. Olivia had asked if Emily wanted to share a room with Patricia, but she declined claiming that Patricia snored much too loudly and she wished to sleep during the night. The woman merely smiled and showed her the room next door.

All the women were given rooms across the hall from the few remaining girls. The tiny rooms reminded Catherine of when she lived at the convent; Emily was reminded of the time she spent at a dormitory when she attended college one year.

As Emily snuggled down in bed and tried not to think of Teri, she wondered what the girls were doing opposite her. She tried to remember when she was young and wild. In those days, she had dated Ashley on and off. She loved her very much and probably would have done anything for her. She couldn't help but laugh when she remembered the times they had spent together when they were younger. She still loved Ashley, though the times and her love had changed to something deeper and more forgiving. Memories chased each other as Emily fell into a soft and inviting sleep.

Patricia couldn't keep her mind away from thoughts of Olivia Michaels. There was something wrong about the whole situation here. Something terribly wrong. The woman wasn't much older than herself, and yet the deep lines on her face lied about her age.

Patricia wished that she could read auras the way Emily could. She was certain that many tales could be told about people from reading the auras that surround them. Instead, she used her psychic abilities to weed out the possibilities. She had seen this kind of illness before. It was not a sickness that a doctor could prescribe pills for.

Although Patricia believed in a great many occult things, she had trouble accepting the concept of witchcraft. To her, witchcraft, along with demonology, was an area that she didn't fuss in. In her superstitious mind, Patricia believed that to acknowledge the reality of it left herself open to curses and hexes. All one had to do was believe. She shivered as she considered the possibilities.

Across the hall, two girls who shared a room together giggled in the dark. The thinner girl propped her head up with her hand and watched her friend in the moonlight that bathed their room. "I'm as serious as a heart attack," she said defensively.

"Give me a break, Stephanie," her friend said, shaking her head. She was sitting with her legs crossed on her own bed.

"I swear he wrote to me and said that he would come up here in a couple of days. He said he was bringing a friend, so I'm supposed to get one of my friends to come along." Stephanie crossed her fingers and hoped that she could convince Jackie to go with her. She didn't want to sneak out alone after lights out, but she really wanted to meet her boyfriend and go to a kegger with him.

Jackie didn't need any more convincing. She knew that she would go without any arm tugging at all, but she also knew that Stephanie was too afraid to go by herself. It was a fun game of manipulation that she played. She had learned the skill at an early age and had become what she considered a pro at it. It was the only way that she knew to get the things that she wanted without having to ask for them. "I don't know. What if we get caught? Or worse yet, what if those people come back and Amanda takes a pot shot at one of us?"

Stephanie waved her hand. "Get off it, will you? God, that happened while we were gone home on a weekend pass. Besides, it hasn't happened again since we've been back."

"Well, join the real world, Stephanie. It still happened. A lot of really creepy things have been happening around here. You remember what happened to Christine, don't you?" Jackie felt a little less manipulative as she remembered her schoolmate. A subtle fear passed over her that made her crawl under her covers for protection.

"Now who's not in the real world, Jackie? Christine was a nut. She has nothing to do with us. We're just going to go out for a little fun and excitement, that's all." Though her words could have convinced anyone that she was not afraid, Stephanie felt a chill run through her at the mention of what had happened to Christine. The memory was still clear in her mind.

"I'll think about it, okay?" Jackie said as she yawned and checked her bedside clock. It was already one in the morning, and the girls were expected to rise at seven and be down in the dining room by seven-thirty in order to start classes at eight.

Ashley woke to a strange sound in the room. It didn't take long for her eyes to clear as sleep quickly left her. In horror she stared at the scene before her.

Someone had strung a rope from the rafter above and tied a slipknot in it. Dangling from the rope was the body of a young girl. Illuminated in the moonlight, below the grizzly scene, was a footstool that lay on its side. The girl was nude.

Quickly, Ashley jumped from the bed and ran to

the girl. Before Ashley could reach her, the scene faded into the shadows of the room.

"Jesus!" Ashley cursed as she came to rest on her bed. She reached for the bedside lamp. Catherine stirred and woke to the bright light.

"What is it?" Catherine asked, seeing the wan color on Ashley's face.

All that Ashley could muster was, "One of the girls killed herself in this room."

SIX

Amanda was up by five. She had barely been able to sleep without waking from dreams about Danielle. She wondered what the coming day would hold in store for her.

As she stepped out into the crisp morning air, she stopped to enjoy the sunrise as it peeked over the mountaintops. She loved the silence of the morning here and lived for it. She had forgotten the filth of the city she had been forced to leave behind years ago. She didn't miss it at all. The only things that mattered to her were the ranch, her mother, and now, Danielle. Years ago it would have been different, but she hardly thought about those times now.

She took another sip from her insulated mug of coffee, sweetened lightly with sugar and creamer, before she stepped off the porch.

In the barn, she found the bucket she used every morning to milk the cow. She tapped the bucket several times and waited. It had become a ritual for her and the five cats that lived in the barn. Lazily, the mother cat strolled out from her warm place in the hay followed by her small brood. "Let's go, momma, breakfast time." The cat rubbed against Amanda's legs and purred loudly.

With the cow milked and the cat fed, Amanda turned the horses out into the corral. She heaved a fresh bale of hay inside the fence and broke it open. The oldest horse came to her and nuzzled her hand. Amanda petted the nose until it nickered and sniffed her pockets. She laughed. "I know what you want, my friend," she said as she pulled some sugar cubes from her pocket. The horse ate quickly from her hand and sniffed her pocket again. Apparently satisfied that Amanda was not holding out on her, the horse turned away and sauntered to the hay pile to eat.

Her last and least favorite chore of the morning, Amanda stopped at the chicken coop and gathered eggs. The chickens were awake and ready to run outside when she opened the door. She waited until all of them were outside before she went in. She never knew what she would find there in the morning. No matter how she tried to keep the predators out, they always found a way in.

One morning she had been greeted by a skunk

that refused to be hurried away from its morning meal of fresh eggs. Another morning she had found a raccoon dining on the carcass of a dead chicken.

Carefully, she stepped in. Nothing seemed to be amiss, and she quickly went about collecting the eggs from the day before. She was pleased to find several dozen lying in the nests.

"Good morning, love," Olivia greeted Amanda as she stepped into the kitchen.

"Morning, Mother," Amanda said as she handed the milk to her mother and carefully set the eggs in the sink to be washed.

Olivia sighed heavily. "I hope you're still not mad at me for inviting the young ladies here. I just thought they could help with our troubles."

Amanda checked the eggs as she washed and set them in the cartons to dry. She shrugged. "I guess it really doesn't matter. I don't think they'll really make a difference, other than to suck away the rest of the money that we have set aside to keep this place running."

"Honey, please try to understand. I want this place to stay open as badly as you do. That's why I wrote Emily and asked her to come." Olivia pleaded with her daughter, hoping that she would be able to read the thoughts that stood behind her words. She was afraid. She knew that if something didn't change soon, she would not be around long enough to worry about the ranch.

"Whatever you believe is best, Mother. I just wish that you had told me, that's all." Amanda snapped the lid of one of the cartons shut. She knew they had reached the end of their options, and she also hoped that the women could make a difference.

Olivia smiled. "If I had told you, would you have approved?"

Amanda grinned at the thought. "Probably not." Turning to her mother with a worried look on her face she added, "I wish sometimes that Dad was still alive. The place really ran smoothly while he was here."

A pained look shadowed Olivia's face for a moment. "I wish that he was, too, but you're your father's daughter. You have his blood running through you, and I'm sure that wherever he is right now, he's looking down with pride and smiling."

Amanda kissed her mother's forehead and hugged her. "I love you, Ma, you know that. If you think that this will work, then we'll try it out. If it doesn't, we haven't lost anything, right?"

"Right," Olivia agreed, though her voice lacked any conviction. She knew that everything would be lost if this didn't work, so she made herself believe that it would all be right in the end.

"By the way," Olivia called to her daughter's back as she left the kitchen, "they're not charging us anything to be here."

Amanda stopped for a moment and thought before she moved on through the door. Her respect for the feisty woman she had confronted yesterday morning went up considerably. For the first time, she felt hope.

* * * * *

Ashley and Catherine had stayed awake until almost five in the morning before they fell back asleep. They had discussed their thoughts on the suicide that Ashley had been witness to. No ideas as to why the girl committed such a desperate act came to them, but it allowed Ashley to talk it out until sleep came to her.

They did not hear Emily when she first tapped on their door at six-thirty. It wasn't until seven-thirty that Catherine rose and answered the knock in a half-awake state.

"Holy cow," Emily commented as she noted Catherine's disheveled hair. "You look like you spent the night out on the town."

Catherine leaned heavily on the door frame and mumbled, "Ashley saw a ghost last night."

Emily laughed heartily. "If I was anyone else, I would send you two to the head doctor. It's time for breakfast, so if you want to, wake up sleeping beauty and come downstairs. We have a long day ahead of us."

Catherine yawned, "Okay, I'll see what I can do."

By the time Ashley and Catherine appeared in the dining room, breakfast was over. Emily and Patricia were sitting at the large table chatting over a cup of coffee.

Olivia rose when she saw the pair enter. Ashley raised her hand. "Please don't bother getting up." Olivia sat, grateful for the rest. Her whole body ached, and she felt quite tired.

"I heard that you girls had quite a time of it last night. I feel terrible, but I had no idea the room was haunted." Olivia felt strange talking about such things and, in another time, she would have laughed at the idea. Now, she knew there were things that could not be explained. Shadows of days gone by moved in front of her bedroom window every few days when the night was just right.

"I was explaining to Emily that a few months ago one of the girls committed suicide in her room late one night. By the time we found her, she had been dead for some time. I didn't tell you because I didn't think it would be important." Olivia turned her gaze to her coffee cup. The pain on her face was enough to tell a whole story.

Ashley accepted a steaming mug of coffee from Patricia. She tried to gather her thoughts before she asked any questions. "Mrs. Michaels, I believe that everything that has happened is connected in some bizarre way. I can't explain exactly what I mean. It is just a feeling I have in my gut, but I don't think the girl committed suicide."

Olivia gasped. "Of course she did. She was not happy here, and she killed herself."

Catherine touched the distraught woman's hand. "What can you tell us about the history of the land that this school was built on?"

The woman relaxed with the change of subject. "This land has been in my husband's family for years. He inherited it from his great uncle who died a number of years back. Sam never really said too much about the land other than he thought at one time someone in his family tried to mine here but died when the mine shaft caved in."

Emily raised her brows. "Do you think that the vision that you see sometimes has anything to do with the people who lived here before?"

Olivia shrugged. "I suppose, dear. I don't really know, but there is someone who might know. A woman who lives on the other side of Sachet is kind of the town historian. She has got to be close to a hundred years old from what I hear, though no one has ever really seen her much. Her name is Bethany O'Connor."

Patricia perked. "Do you have any idea where she lives?" The idea of talking with someone that old and with that much history peaked her curiosity.

Olivia rose from her chair nodding. She reentered the room with a piece of paper on which there was sketched a map with directions. "This is a hand drawn map by the woman herself. She sent it to my husband the first week we moved here. On the other side is the note that went with it. I don't know why Sam never went to see her, and I never really asked him about it."

Patricia turned the old piece of parchment over and tried to read the faded writing. She read it aloud.

Samuel Michaels:
I must see you soon. It is imperative that we meet. I sense that you and your kin are in great danger.

Bethany O'Connor

"And your husband never went to see this woman?" Patricia knit her brows with concern. She wondered at the strange note that was almost thirty years old. Olivia seemed to show no care at all with the note.

"Olivia, how did your husband die?" Patricia asked brashly.

A bewildered expression crossed the woman's face. "What does that have to do with anything?"

Patricia shrugged. "I was just wondering. It seems strange that a woman you don't know would send a warning to your husband the first week that you moved here."

Olivia sighed as though the burden of the memory were enough to force the rest of the waning life out of her. "He died of a heart attack a year ago."

Patricia nodded. She wore an expression of sympathy while she churned the fact around in her mind. She knew that sometime today she would be in contact with this O'Connor woman. There was something to the warning. She could feel the paper humming ever so slightly with an emotion that thirty years ago must have been very strong. The feeling was fear. Extreme fear.

Amanda was waiting when Danielle pulled into the driveway. She threw her fishing rod and tackle box in the back of the truck and hopped up into the cab. Danielle smiled at her as she pulled the gears into reverse. It was the sweetest smile Amanda had ever seen.

"Morning," Danielle said as she moved out to the road that would lead the women through Sachet.

Amanda grinned. She was about to spend the entire day with one of the most beautiful women she had ever known in her adult life. Butterflies fluttered in her stomach as she wondered what the events of the day would lead to. The farther the two women drove from the ranch, the less she thought of the troubles that plagued her and her mother. In her mind, she claimed this day as her own and would not allow anything else in.

Danielle ran her hand through her shoulder-length, dark blonde hair. "I hope that we catch something today," she said, turning to watch Amanda gaze out the window. She was hoping that Amanda would look her way. She loved the pale blue color of her eyes. No matter what other reason she had for asking Amanda to join her fishing, she knew it would give her an opportunity to lose herself in those eyes for a while.

Amanda could feel Danielle watching her. It made her self-conscious and a bit uneasy. She wondered what Danielle could possibly be looking at. Amanda was the first to admit that she was nothing special and, in fact, she had inherited her father's looks. While her mother had been a beauty when she was younger, her father was at best ruggedly handsome. Amanda had gotten his red hair and penetrating, pale blue eyes. She considered them her only redeeming features, though she had been told when she was younger that she was quite a woman to look at. But, most of the people who had told her that had been high on drugs.

Danielle grinned as the pair bounced around in the truck cab. "You look like you are a million miles away."

Amanda turned her eyes to the other woman. For a moment, she saw an expression pass over her face, but before she could identify what it was it disappeared. "I was just thinking about the past, nothing important. I have to be honest, I have really been looking forward to this. I hardly slept last night. It has been a long time since I have been off the ranch."

Danielle touched her hand briefly as she said, "I've been looking forward to it, too."

The place where Danielle had touched her tingled. Amanda longed for her touch again. It had been so long that she had almost forgotten those desires that she had buried when she came to Idaho. She thought that she had successfully burned those bridges when her lover was killed in a street fight. At the time she was seventeen and thought she owned the world. She shrugged off the feelings of the past. This was now, and Danielle was not Karrie.

Olivia fought hard not to show the pain from severe stomach cramps as she walked to one of the classrooms. In the room next to her own was a teacher who had been retired from the public school district a few years when Olivia persuaded her to come and teach here.

Olivia paused as she passed by the closed door of the room. Allison was scratching numbers on the blackboard, and her students were copying the figures. Allison was the only other teacher who remained at the school after admissions started to drop. She had told Olivia that she would teach for nothing if it came to that.

Olivia opened the door to her own classroom and

sat at the desk. She had hoped the antacid taken earlier would have eased the cramps, but so far her hopes were in vain.

She tried to convince herself that the pain was not as bad as it was earlier. After what seemed like an eternity, she began to believe herself. Perhaps, she thought, what she had eaten earlier didn't sit well with her.

From her wire basket that sat on one corner of her desk she pulled out some papers. She knew she would have to have the tests corrected by the time she got the girls in the afternoon.

Olivia found her red pen in her desk drawer and went to work on the paper that lay in front of her. Off in the furthest part of her mind, she thought about her husband, Sam. She wondered why he had never gone to see the woman who wrote to him and why he had never told her about the imploring note on the other side. It wasn't until after his death that she found the note and map.

She had heard of Bethany O'Connor and of her rather unusual past times. People in small communities tended to be unkind to those who went against their own folkways. From what Olivia could remember, people shunned her because the woman practiced the ancient art of witchcraft.

Olivia shivered at the thoughts that ran through her mind and went back to correcting the papers on her desk.

SEVEN

Emily and Patricia set out shortly after breakfast to find O'Connor. They had got lost several times and had to backtrack to find their way around the narrow roads of the countryside.

At one point, the women drove a treacherous, curvy road that wound around a mountainside. Because both women were from the city, neither knew how the drive the dirt road that confronted them. After a while, Emily decided to backtrack for the third time since they had started out. About a quarter mile up the road, she discovered, finally, what looked like a wagon trail. Carefully, she slipped the front end of the car into the muddy ruts.

As Emily maneuvered the car to back out again, Patricia glanced out the window in time to see a huge black dot in the road ahead. The black dot moved closer, and Patricia swallowed hard to push back her panic. "Uh, Emily, I don't mean to bug you, dear, but can you please move the car faster?" Patricia asked, her eyes growing bigger as the dot moved closer to the vehicle.

Emily looked up in time to see a huge black bear closing in on their vehicle. Both women screamed in unison. Emily put the car in reverse and floored the accelerator. The rear wheels of the car spun helplessly in the mud.

The bear sauntered closer to the strange vehicle and drew itself on two feet as it sniffed the air.

Emily threw the car into drive, then quickly into reverse, trying to persuade the car to rock out of the ruts. The second time she did this, the car lurched and sped backward off the trail until it was again on the dirt road.

Both women bounced forward when Emily hit the brakes. Without a second thought or a look back, Emily threw the car into drive and sped down the road.

The bear followed the car as far as the road. A moment later a woman with white hair stood next to the bear. She heard the car speeding down the road away from her.

She spoke softly to the bear and fed it a few huckleberries out of a cloth sack that hung at her side. She knew who the women were and what they sought. She had seen this a moment before the women turned onto her road, but she was too late to keep Keva from frightening them off. The woman shrugged. They would be back, and she would be more prepared the next time they came.

When she stepped out of the quiet school, Ashley found Catherine stroking the muzzle of one of the horses. She watched a moment as Catherine talked to the horse. Ashley marveled at the woman who was now her lover.

It had been a long journey to find the most perfect love in her life. She had more than given up on love when Catherine walked into her life and turned her heart inside out. Ashley slid her arm around her lover's waist. "Hey, babe, feel like taking a walk?"

The horse snorted and sauntered away from the fence. "Sure," Catherine said as a smile crossed her lips. Ashley longed to kiss her, but she held herself in check for fear someone might be watching them. She didn't dare risk a run-in with Amanda, though Ashley sensed that similar fires burned within Amanda for a woman named Danielle.

As the pair walked slowly from the corral, Ashley thought out loud. "Emily said something about an old cabin being on the grounds somewhere, but I'll be damned if I can see it anywhere from our window upstairs."

Catherine shrugged. She hadn't given it much thought. Her mind was more focused on the story she had heard from Emily about a certain run-in with witches. She wondered if the group had ever bothered to come back and what they had wanted. She had been gathering all of the information that she had ever read about witches in her mind. Most, she believed, had been given a bad reputation by the few who waded into the blacker waters of the craft. While there were those who practiced from the darker side of the spectrum, there were also those who used their unique talents for healing.

"I have been thinking about the mine. I am getting some of the weirdest feelings from it," Catherine said as they approached the boards that walled the mouth of the shaft. She closed her eyes and touched the boards. Instantly, her thoughts were invaded with visions of the past. In still, snapshotlike photographs, they came to her.

The beams that supported part of the ceiling had given in. Two people were trapped. A feeling of fear invaded her senses. "Run," a voice shouted. And then, nothingness. All was still as the last of the earth and small rocks slid down the blockade at the mouth of the mine.

Catherine jerked her hand away quickly. Her eyes snapped open, and for a moment she had trouble realizing the thoughts that were her own. "Are you all right?" Ashley asked.

Catherine nodded. "Someone died in the mine when it caved in."

Ashley listened as she led her partner away from the mouth of the cavern. Visions that came from the past or ones that spoke of the future always seemed to drain Catherine for a few minutes. Apparently it was necessary for Catherine to give a part of her life force to those who had none in order for her to see living pictures from the past.

"The strangest thing was that I saw the face of

the woman who died there," Catherine said, stopping for a moment.

"Why is that so strange?" Ashley asked, her voice mimicking the confusion on her face.

"She looked like Amanda," Catherine said.

Quickly, Ashley asked, "Did you see something from the future?"

Catherine shook her head. "I don't know. I couldn't stay with it that long."

Danielle pulled the emergency brake on the truck and turned the ignition off. "Here we are," she announced with a smile on her face.

Amanda took in the forest as it unfolded before her. The pines of deep green shadowed the forest floor of various foliage that thrived in the shade. Tiny flowers dotted the landscape. Amanda recognized some of the broad-leaved plants as thistleberry, which grew large, red berries. Other bushes she knew grew huckleberries.

She opened the cab door of the truck and met Danielle with her fishing pole a few yards away. The women started walking together up a deer trail that led to a creek beyond.

Not too far from where Amanda was rigging her pole with a hook and a few sinkers, Danielle found an ideal deep hole in the running water. She dropped in her line a foot above the hole and allowed the rushing water to carry the bait into it. It was only a matter of minutes before she felt a tug. Carefully, she pulled the line with one hand while the other guided the pole to the bank of the creek. She was pleased to see a seven-inch brook trout flopping on the ground.

"Damn," Amanda commented as she passed by. Danielle grinned as she watched Amanda. With half her attention devoted to the fish, she watched Amanda work farther down the creek. She was attracted to Amanda, but she had not planned on it going beyond that. Her feelings troubled her. She averted her eyes and concentrated on the fish in her hands.

Olivia made it through her afternoon classes and retired to her room. The pains in her stomach had faded, leaving her more fatigued than ever. For a long time she lay on her bed staring at the ceiling, waiting for sleep.

She wasn't sure of the time when she woke, but the walls of her room had blackened with the night. From very far away, she heard a woman screaming in pain. Olivia rose from her bed and followed the sounds. She found herself, suddenly, inside the tiny cabin that she had seen before when the shades from the past came to visit her.

An orange firelight burned in a large, open fireplace and danced on the walls. A woman came through a door that hung on squeaky hinges. Her strong, soft features were tight with tension as she moved purposely around the room gathering a washbasin and a few towels. The woman wiped her brow with her hand and sighed under her teeth, "Where is that woman?"

A small boy rushed through the front door, followed by a plump woman who looked to be in her thirties.

"Lord, am I glad to see you," the woman said, carrying the washbasin back into the room from which she had come. The plump woman addressed the boy before she followed, her voice kind and soft as she instructed, "You stay here, Jacob, and tend to the fire, just like we planned, okay?"

The boy nodded as his eyes, wide with concern, rested on the doorway where beyond a woman cried in pain. The woman bustled in and shut the door behind her. Muffled sounds of voices could be heard as the two women moved here and there behind the door.

Behind the door a woman in labor lay on the bed. The dark-haired woman was talking softly while she soothed the forehead of her friend with a damp cloth.

The plump woman spoke sternly, "Push, Alex. One more time. That's it, child, push."

The redheaded woman rose partially from the bed. Her face was flushed, and a fine sheen of perspiration glittered in the lamplight.

Olivia stepped back. The woman resembled Amanda. Her head spun and she felt faint. Feverishly, she tried to reason with her disoriented mind.

A baby cried as the plump woman cleansed the tiny body and spoke in hushed tones. She wrapped the child in a warm blanket and brought the child to her mother. "It's a girl," she said, smiling.

Alex turned her face from the child and wept. The woman that sat at her side took the baby in her arms and cuddled it. The child quieted at her touch. "She's beautiful, Alex," the woman pleaded through her tears.

"I don't care, Eliza, take this child from me now, I

beg you," the mother pleaded. There was pain in the heavy Irish brogue.

Eliza looked from Alex to the plump woman, who was busily massaging Alex's lower abdomen. For a moment the two women said nothing as their eyes met.

The midwife sighed, "It doesn't matter how the child came into this world, my friend, but she will need a mother to care for her now."

Alex caught a glimpse of the child out of the corner of her eye. Slowly, she turned her head. A wispy smile touched her lips as she reached to touch the small patch of red hair that crowned the tiny head.

Olivia, still disoriented, felt herself being pulled away from the room. Slowly, the cabin faded as she retreated from it.

All was dark, and a curious void enveloped her mind. She could feel herself waking. When she opened her eyes, she was greeted by the shadows of late afternoon as they lazily hung in her room.

Olivia rose from her bed. She felt very drained. The dream had enervated her tiny reserve of strength. She contemplated its meaning and made a note to talk to Emily about it when she saw her again. She knew the dream was significant; she just didn't know to what degree.

Danielle stretched out her legs next to the fire and rolled the fish they had caught in tinfoil with a touch of butter and salt. She shoved the wrapped fish into the coals she had scraped to one side.

Amanda sat staring into the flames as the sun crept to the final stages of the day. She could not believe that the day had escaped so quickly. Silently, she chewed on a weed she plucked up next to her and thought about the day.

"You're awfully quiet," Danielle commented. She leaned back on her elbows and stretched to her full height. Her eyes watched the woman who sat near her staring into the flames of the small fire.

Amanda smiled. "Sorry. I was just thinking about the day and wondering how I should go about asking you if you wanted to so something tomorrow." Her heart pounded in her chest and she hoped that her face didn't flush too bad.

A smile touched the woman's face. "What did you have in mind?" She poked the fire with a long stick.

Amanda shrugged. "Maybe go to Spokane or something." Her throat felt dry. It had been a long time since she had been out with anyone, let alone a woman. She focused her eyes on the fire and steeled herself for a possible rejection.

Danielle fought with herself in the silence that had fallen between the two women. Her heart was leading her far away from the path she had to follow. "Sure," she said before her head could change the answer.

Amanda let the breath out slowly. Her whole body tingled with the possibilities of tomorrow. She smiled to herself as her thoughts ran madly around her mind. She already knew where they would go and what they would do if it was left up to her.

EIGHT

Olivia looked like she had seen death up close and had barely lived to talk about it. Ashley searched her face as she sat at the table. She wasn't sure if she had heard her, so she asked again, "Olivia, are you all right? Would you like me to drive you to the hospital or something?"

This time, Olivia's eyes fluttered up and gazed at Ashley. Olivia shrugged, then shook her head. "I have some special tea that seems to help my condition. I'll be fine in a minute or so."

Ashley touched the woman's hand briefly. She

could feel the woman's sickness as it radiated off her skin. Ashley flinched as Olivia pulled away. The pain was intense, and the waves of nausea that swept through her body made her throat burn. Ashley knew Olivia belonged in the hospital, but she wasn't sure how to convince her of that. She would talk to Amanda about it when she saw her next.

Catherine pinched her forehead in worry. She had not missed the look on Ashley's face when she touched Olivia, and she felt useless in the face of the woman's torture.

After a few minutes of silence, the color returned to Olivia's face and her eyes lost some of the dullness. As Olivia began to speak, her voice regained some of its freshness. "I had the strangest dream this afternoon. It seemed so real . . ."

As Ashley listened to the story, her own experiences of dream-walking into the past pulled at her senses. She remembered a fear that she thought she had put to rest. She could still see the mansion on the cliffs in Astoria as though she were there in the flesh. She wondered if her life would ever be absent the horror she had lived through there. She pulled her mind back and left the past to itself as Olivia finished her story.

Olivia felt like a fool. A smile softly touched her worn features as her thin hand came to her forehead. "I guess it sounds crazy," she said, looking from one woman to the other.

Catherine glanced at Ashley. Ashley could see that Catherine also remembered the days they had spent in the old Windlow mansion. She shook her head, "It doesn't sound crazy to me. A while back I had some similar experiences with dream-walking. It can be frightening in the beginning, but after a while you just get used to it."

"I hope that I don't have to get used to it," Olivia said. "I really don't want to have another one of those — what did you call it? — dream-walking experiences." Her face set in determination, Olivia looked at Ashley, but Ashley's eyes told another story. Ashley knew that once the dreams started, there would be no end until the power causing the visions was laid to rest.

Ashley thought for a moment that she had seen the aura that surrounded Olivia. The aura was a deep brown, almost black. Death stood very near the woman, and Ashley swore she could feel a cold whoosh of air.

With an air of excitement, Emily and Patricia entered the dining room. Both women were talking so fast that Ashley wondered how they were able to communicate with each other.

Patricia's bright red hair, which had been pulled up in a combination of pins and combs that morning, had come unfastened and lay across her shoulders. Her clothes were crumpled from her sitting in a hot car for most of the day.

Ashley looked both women up and down before she asked, "What's the commotion about? Did you find that Bethany woman?"

The women looked at Ashley. After a few seconds of dead silence, both began talking at once as they settled in the chairs around the table.

Catherine raised her hand, and an amused smile

touched her lips. "Hang on, ladies, one at a time." Ashley laughed aloud as the tension at the table broke.

Olivia smiled in amusement. She liked Emily and had found a longed for friend in Patricia. She wished that she had Patricia's energy, but it evaded her like a butterfly that fluttered away in the summertime winds.

Patricia pursed her lips and put a hand on Emily's arm. Ashley knew that her mother was preparing to tell some harrowing talk about their adventure. She leaned back in her chair and listened.

Patricia began at the beginning even though everyone at the table knew what had happened before the pair left the house. Finally, Patricia told about running into the bear. Emily could not help but add her own statements as Patricia talked. Their eyes were wide with excitement as they told of their "near death experience."

Ashley laughed. "God, Mother, it was just a bear. He was probably more frightened of you than you were of him."

Olivia smiled. "I imagine that the bears are used to cars going up there. People pick huckleberries and hunt there all the time. I have never heard of anyone being hurt by bears up there. He was probably just curious," Olivia added as she swallowed the last of her tea.

Catherine nodded in agreement, though she knew absolutely nothing about bears.

"Well, Emily and I decided to go up there again tomorrow if anyone cares to join us. But in the meantime, I think that I had better freshen up. I look a mess," Patricia said as she tried hopelessly to pull her hair back into the style she had it in earlier.

Olivia nodded and pushed her chair up to the table. "I suppose that I had better do so as well. It is near supper time, and I imagine that the girls are going to be pretty hungry when they come in." She followed closely behind Patricia, but found it hard to keep up. It wasn't until Olivia was at the top of the stairs that she saw Patricia again. She barely had enough breath to ask, "Patricia, may I speak with you a moment, please?"

Patricia turned and rested her gaze on Olivia. Olivia looked like death itself as she stood stooping slightly in the late afternoon shadows. Patricia's heart ached for her. "Sure," she said moving away from her door. She followed Olivia to her apartment.

Emily wandered the grounds of the old school until she found herself near the old mine. She had been thinking about Teri. There was something so sweet and so shy about her. She remembered the last time Teri had touched her. Emily's heart fluttered and her body tingled with excitement as her mind recalled every detail. The kiss, the touch, the feel of Teri's body as it melted with her own, the feeling of oneness.

Emily's knees grew weak. She sat down on a large stone in front of the mine. A wave of fear and pain that felt like an electrical shock pulsed from the rock into her body. With a jolt, Emily pulled away from her thoughts. The emission flowed through her arms and engulfed her entire being. Never, in all her years as a practicing psychic, had she felt anything like it. She fought to pull herself away from the rock, but she sensed it would not readily release her.

After a few minutes, images flooded her mind. The impressions flew by so fast that she could not see any one thing clearly. She shivered as if a cold wind had just touched her skin. Something terrible was about to happen here. Something very painful. Her thoughts formed in broken sentences and impressions. At the very end, she saw the face of a woman. And she saw Teri.

Weakly, Emily pulled away from the rock. She felt drained. It had taken most of her energy for the stone to reveal what was to be.

"Something terrible is going to happen," Emily said. Ashley stood at the window of her room and looked down on the mine. She had felt it too. Something had spoken to her in brief impressions and screamed in terror.

Ashley pulled her gaze from the mine. When she looked at Emily, Ashley's face reflected the fear that she could not hide. "I felt something out there, too, though I never told anyone. I thought that perhaps the event has already occurred and had left an impression there."

Emily shook her head. "It is something that hasn't happened yet. I can feel it. So much pain and fear. My God, it was like being on a roller coaster of emotion. I'm afraid. I saw Teri's face the very last thing."

Ashley moved from the window. She touched her friend's arm. "Teri isn't even here, so you can put that fear to rest. You know as well as I do that the things we see that belong to the future are not written in stone."

Emily shot a glance at her friend. Ashley raised her hand and smiled. "Hold on, I didn't mean to make a bad pun. I only wanted you to remember that things don't always come out of the way we see them. The past is unchangeable, but the future can be altered. That's why we're here, to give the future a chance to change."

Emily smiled, though deep down she could not dismiss her feeling of utter doom. Something was going to happen. She was just grateful that Teri was tucked safely away in Portland.

Stephanie and Jackie sat in class and passed notes back and forth when Mrs. Stewart's back was turned. The three other girls in the classroom watched the teacher intently as the woman scratched facts on the board.

Stephanie rolled her eyes and mouthed the word *bookworms* with a sour look on her face and nodded her head toward the other girls. Jackie smiled as she eyed them. She missed the other students who had come to stay here before all of the weird stuff started. She was getting tired of Stephanie. She was so predictable and so easy to manipulate that she was no longer a challenge.

Jackie's mind turned to the women who stayed down the hall from her bedroom. She thought about Emily who had argued with Amanda. *That one would be a challenge,* she thought as she copied a few notes from the board. She knew from the first day that the other two women who came with Emily were lesbians. It made her stomach feel funny as she thought about it.

Quickly, she drew her mind away from the pictures that came to her when she explored the word *lesbian.* The pictures frightened her and stirred other emotions that she kept well hidden, even from herself.

Jackie allowed a mental image of Emily to pass through her mind, and she held on to it for a moment as though it were a photograph. At her own will, she let the image fade. *What games I could play with this one,* she thought as a feeling of joy spread from her stomach to her face. It was warm and it tingled inside her. She made a mental note to seek her out later and talk to her. Learning the way that someone ticked, Jackie reasoned, was the first and hardest step. The rest would follow through easily behind that.

She passed a note back to Stephanie with something she had halfheartedly scrawled on it. She faded back into her mind to work out the fine details she would need for later.

* * * * *

70

Emily felt eyes on her at the dinner table. She looked up in time to see Jackie look away from her. At first she was amused with the game but, after the twentieth time, she lost interest. Emily wished Teri were here. Emily wondered how she could continue these missions of mercy without the woman she loved at her side. She had hoped that Teri would have showed up by now. She would call her tomorrow just to hear her voice.

Jackie sensed when enough was enough, and she quit staring at the woman who sat across from her. She tried to concentrate on what Stephanie was saying to Mrs. Michaels and fought to keep her eyes to herself. She knew that she had gotten Emily's attention. She also knew there would be time later. She had memorized the women's schedules and knew them by heart. She dabbed the cloth napkin to her lips and smiled at Stephanie.

Ashley sat next to the plump girl named Jackie. From the moment she sat down, she began fighting strange feelings. She sat still and tried to concentrate on the vibes that filled the air. She knew that the child was up to no good, and after having caught a few glimpses that Jackie shot to Emily, Ashley thought she knew what was going on. Later, she would have to talk to Emily about the girl who seemed to have a crush on her.

Amanda tried hard to sit still. She felt as though she had sprouted wings and was flying around the room high above the dining table. Her concentration was shot. Her mind kept returning to a kiss. A sweet, passionate kiss that she hoped would not be long in coming. A kiss that she wished to share with Danielle. Over and over in her mind, she watched the different scenarios that were possible. Each one was sweeter than the one before, and soon blood was rushing to her head and her face was flushing.

"Dear, are you feeling all right?" Olivia asked, touching her daughter's hand. "You have barely eaten anything."

Amanda nodded. "I think I'm just a little tired, that's all. I'll excuse myself and head on up to my room."

Patricia watched Amanda leave. She had seen that look on Ashley's face a dozen times in the past and knew what was going on. Her gaze fell on Olivia. She mentally replayed the conversation she had with her earlier.

Over a steaming mug of coffee, Olivia shared her fears about her daughter. Patricia listened intently for almost an hour as the woman went from tears to smiles and back to tears again. Her heart was being pulled in two directions.

"My daughter ran with a girl named Karrie when she was younger. I tried really hard to make myself believe they were just friends, but after a while I knew there was something else to it. Amanda never brought home any boys or dated. She only hung around with this rough looking girl. I'm afraid it's starting all over again with this woman named Danielle. I tried to bring her up right, you know. I nurtured her and did all those things that Doctor Spock recommended. I feel that I've failed her." The woman sobbed for a moment, then she dabbed her eyes with a Kleenex. Olivia looked pleadingly at

Patricia for some answer, some solution, or some advice on what to do with her daughter.

Patricia sighed and took the woman's hand in her own. "Listen, I went through this with my daughter. Oh, yes, my daughter's a lesbian," Patricia said as Olivia gaped at her.

"What did you do?" Olivia asked with interest. She trusted this loud, reflective woman who sat on her couch. It had been a long time since she had been able to talk to anyone her own age.

Patricia shrugged, "I finally decided to let her live her own life. God only knows, she doesn't want to live mine. I have to admit that I don't completely understand it, but it is what she chooses to do with her life. I am proud of my daughter, and her sexual preference is such a small part of what makes her a whole woman."

Olivia nodded and clung to the woman's words as though they were pearls of wisdom.

Since her afternoon talk with Patricia, Olivia had thought about her daughter. When the family had moved here, Amanda had become another person entirely. Olivia was proud of her daughter and loved her with all her heart. Perhaps Patricia was right. It was Amanda's life, and she needed to live it the way that she saw fit.

Now, as she watched her daughter leave the room, Olivia knew that it was time to let her go. Amanda had to live her own life, not that of her mother. Olivia sighed audibly.

* * * * *

Catherine sat quietly as she mulled several thoughts in her mind. She was trying to make the pieces fit the puzzle. She knew there must be a correlation between what she had seen in the mine and what Olivia had seen in her dream. Most probably, she decided, the women who played out a small piece of their lives in front of Olivia were the same women whom Catherine had seen in the mine.

Catherine concentrated on both images. She mentally flashed from one to the other until they ran together. She decided that the images were the same. The only thing that stumped her was the deep familiarity between Amanda, the woman in the mine, and the mother in Olivia's dream. There were several ways of finding out for sure. She knew that Emily would break an ankle to do it, but what concerned her was that Ashley would break an ankle to have no part in it. Weighing all the options, Catherine resolved it in her mind. She would simply have to find a way to convince Ashley that this was the only way and that she was the only one who could do it.

Danielle stood in front of the old woman as she plucked leaves and bugs out of the huckleberries she had gathered earlier. Keva lay on the floor on her back and snored audibly. Danielle waited for the woman to speak.

After a moment, the old woman raised her sightless eyes to Danielle, a look of concern stitched across her face. "What do you know of the women staying at the Michaels place?" she asked as her hands busily ran through the berries in the kitchen sink.

Danielle shrugged, "Not a whole lot. Amanda said that her mother called them to investigate the strange happenings there. She doesn't have a lot of confidence in what they'll find."

The old woman smiled softly. "She shouldn't be so quick to disregard these women. They came to see me today, but Keva scared them off."

Danielle's face pinched with concern. "When did this happen?"

"Earlier," the old woman said without offering any more information.

Danielle thought for a moment as she paced the floor. The last thing she wanted was people up here snooping around. "What do you think they wanted?"

The old woman began to pack the berries in a large mason jar. She knew what the women had wanted. She had sensed it in the wind. After all of these years of waiting and wondering, Olivia Michaels had sent someone to inquire about the note to her husband. Her heart sank with that knowledge; it was too late now for her to do anything to help them. Her powers had faded, just as the time her red hair had turned white.

The old woman sighed as she sealed the jar. "They came to see if I could help them with their troubles. Many years ago I wrote a letter to Sam Michaels warning him of the danger that his family was in, but he chose to ignore it. Now he's dead, and Olivia is soon to follow him. There is nothing that I can do, now."

Danielle followed the woman out the cabin door

where they sat in a porch swing. The sun was melting over the mountains in a profusion of colors that sent shades of yellow and orange across the hills and touched the cabin walls with its hues.

"Mr. Michaels died of a heart attack a year ago. There was nothing strange about that," Danielle stated. She watched the woman's face as she talked, looking for a hint of what Bethany was thinking.

The old woman touched her fingers to her forehead as though she were in deep thought. She did not respond right away, and Danielle wondered if she had fallen asleep.

The woman's voice startled Danielle out of her thoughts. "Sam didn't die of a heart attack. He was murdered, just as Olivia is going to be murdered but no one will think anything of it. No autopsy will be done, and her body will be laid to rest just as Sam's was. And then they will have won."

Danielle had heard some strange things come from Bethany O'Connor's lips before, but this was too much. Olivia was sick, but Amanda said she thought it was because the cancer had come back again. But Danielle had never known Bethany to be wrong.

"How do you know these things?" Danielle asked, though she already knew what the answer would be. She raised her hand. "Never mind, I know."

The old woman turned to Danielle and said, "Danielle, terrible things are about to happen there. There are people who will do anything it takes to get what they want. People with powers that are beyond even my imagination. I don't know how to stop them. I just don't know."

Despite the warm night, Danielle felt a shiver run

the length of her spine as goose bumps prickled her arms. A fear she had never before seen on her great-grandmother's face clung in the soft wrinkles as an ominous foreboding of something horrible yet to come.

NINE

Shortly after supper, Emily stepped outside to breathe the fresh, evening air. With her arms crossed, she moved off the porch and into the bath of yellow moonlight. She breathed deeply. The scent of sweet pine and horses touched her skin softly. She had walked a few paces away from the school when she heard a voice behind her in the dark.

"Warm night, isn't it?"

Emily whirled around and caught the face of Jackie moving in the shadows. She let the air out of her lungs as the tingle of adrenaline faded in her blood. "You scared the love of God right out of me." She thought about adding *child* at the end but changed her mind. This girl was a long way from being a child.

Jackie smiled. She enjoyed the thrill. She moved closer to Emily. She caught faint whiffs of Emily's perfume. "Sorry," Jackie said, allowing a smile to cross her lips for a moment.

Emily smiled back, though in the back of her mind she sensed danger. She tried to bring the feeling into the light, but it evaded her when Jackie drew near. She let the suspicions go for the moment.

"Are you going on a walk?" Jackie asked innocently.

Emily shrugged, "I was thinking about it. Why?"

Jackie let a pleading expression cross her face. She wanted just enough to draw Emily's attention to her. "I thought that you might allow me to join you. I just get so tired of hanging around with Stephanie and her crazy ways. Besides, I wanted to talk to you about something."

Emily was about ready to send the girl back into the school when Jackie said, "Please, I know some things about Christine that might help you with your investigation." Jackie tried to sound desperate.

Jackie could tell that she almost had Emily's attention, but for good measure she added, "It's stuff that I couldn't even tell the police or Mrs. Michaels."

Bingo, Jackie thought, *I have her.* She had spun the threads for this tale in her mind all day long. As she followed Emily into the night, she began to weave them together.

* * * * *

Catherine had found time earlier to talk with Patricia about her plan, and now the women cornered Ashley at the sink where she stood. Patricia winked at Catherine; she knew she had her daughter where they wanted her, with nowhere to run. And she couldn't argue — Mrs. Michaels was in the kitchen with them.

"Um, Ashley," Catherine began. She saw Ashley's face tense a bit. Ashley knew something was coming. Catherine would have to check herself next time and try a different approach to keep Ashley from suspecting anything.

"What," Ashley asked as she dipped a dinner plate into the rinse water and put it in the rack for her mother to dry.

"We were thinking about something that might help this investigation go a bit faster and, well, we need your help," Catherine said, watching Ashley out of the corner of her eye.

"What," Ashley asked as she scrubbed a large metal pan. Her voice remained monotone. She suspected what was coming, and she dreaded saying no.

"We were thinking about having a seance, and we hoped you would be medium for us," Patricia blurted from behind. She was never one to waste words.

Ashley shook her head. Catherine saw determination on her face. This was going to be a long battle. "Please," Catherine pleaded.

"No, I hate doing those things. You know that. And I especially hate doing it since the time at the Windlow mansion. You're lucky you got me here at all." A stubborn expression crossed Ashley's face at the same time fear stirred deep within her.

"Look, Ashley, all of us are capable mediums and could probably get the job done, but you're one of the best. We need you to help us. Besides, we'll all be there if something goes wrong," Patricia said from behind.

Ashley turned with her jaw set. She was absolutely determined to refuse when she saw Olivia's face. Olivia put an arm on her shoulder and said, "I understand why you don't want to do this. Believe me, I do. I don't want any of you to put your life at risk for me."

Patricia had her brightly painted lips pursed to respond when Ashley put her hand in the air. She had seen something in the face of Olivia. It was something in her eyes that seemed to reflect off her very soul. Ashley smiled, "All right, I'll do it just this once, but never again. Does everybody understand me? Never again." With that, Ashley turned back to the sink to wash the dishes.

When she looked up at the window, Ashley saw her own reflection and someone else's. When she turned, no one was there. The image was that of the woman who looked a lot like Amanda.

"Where's Emily?" Ashley asked as she set a white candle in the middle of a small coffee table. Bewildered, Catherine looked at Patricia, who turned her gaze to Olivia.

Olivia shrugged, "She left about an hour ago on a walk, but I haven't seen her since." Catherine laid an old set of rosary beads at her place around the table. "She's probably okay. We can start without her.

When she comes in, she can join us," she said as she sat cross-legged on the floor.

Patricia looked a little apprehensive. "Maybe we shouldn't do this without all of us here."

Ashley sighed, "Come on, Mother. You're the one who thought this was such a grand idea. Let's get it started before I lose my nerve."

Patricia shot a nervous glance toward the apartment door. Something in the air didn't feel right. Something was out of place when she thought about Emily, and it made her skin tighten with a chill.

Catherine interrupted Patricia's thoughts. "Come on, Pat, I'm sure that Ashley's right. Emily will be in shortly, and she can join us then." Patricia nodded and took her place across from Catherine.

Olivia felt a bit out of place. She wasn't sure if she was supposed to join or leave the room. She had never been to a seance but had heard some things about them. She cleared her throat, "When we first came here, there was a cabin on the grounds. Sam wanted to tear it down, though Amanda and I thought that it was quaint and that we should keep it. Well, one day we both took a walk and sneaked over to the dilapidated old thing. The roof was almost gone, and the floorboards were fairly rotten. We carefully went inside. It looked as though whoever had lived there had left in a hurry or had gone out and never come back to recover their belongings. I am surprised that over time people hadn't taken all of the things we found. But when we made the decision to come here, all we had heard about this piece of land was that it was cursed and that anyone who dared set foot here would die. Anyway, I still have some of the salvageable stuff. Would you like to look at it? It may help with the seance."

"That would be great. It's easier than going in cold. If you have something that still gives off vibrations from the original owner, we may be able to see a lot more," Ashley said excitedly.

Olivia returned with a metal box. Carefully, she inserted a key into the imbedded lock box and opened it. She pulled out the items and laid them across the table. Patricia picked up a long rusty hat pin with a teardrop pearl attached to it. "Look at this thing," Patricia said grinning. "I haven't seen one of these things in a long time. In fact, I was just a girl, and I remember my great grandmother used them. I still have one of her hat pins that she gave me right before she died."

Ashley's attention was drawn to a folding, straightedged, ivory-handled razor. The minute that she touched it, she could feel strong vibrations coming from it. Impressions moved through her mind faster than she could slow them down. She dropped the razor in front of her and looked up wide-eyed.

"What's the matter, babe?" Catherine asked, looking up from an old, chipped china shaving cup.

Ashley smiled shakily. "I think that this will do. The vibrations that are coming off that thing are incredible," Ashley said, touching the razor lightly with her hand. "The best way to do this is to have everyone hold hands with one another. And Mother, you and Catherine touch my arms as I put my hand on the razor. That way we can all see what the spirit wants us to know. Olivia, would you like to join us?"

Olivia started to shake her head but changed her mind. "I would like to join you if you don't mind.

I'm not a psychic or anything. You don't think that I could hinder the — what did you call it? — vibrations?"

Patricia patted the floor next to her. She smiled, "Come on, honey, it's obvious that the spirits find you comfortable; otherwise they would not have communicated as much as they have to you already." Olivia smiled and sank to the floor. She took Patricia and Catherine by the hand.

When she was ready, Ashley touched the razor. "Now, remember," she advised before she became lost in the image that came to her. "Envision the image moving slowly through your mind as though it were a movie, otherwise none of us will see a damned thing."

The huge brick building looked like a mansion. The sun was setting, and the snow reflected brilliant colors of deep reds and fluorescent oranges. Couples milled by casually in winter dress that could have come from the pages of a Sears Roebuck catalog dated 1898.

Off to the northeast corner of the building was a large, frozen pond. A great deal of laughter rose from the throng of people who gathered around the snowbanks edging the ice. Large oil lamps hung from long pegs set deep in the ice around the entire circumference of the pond. On the pond, someone was skating haphazardly, though with great skill. A billing in a woman's hand announced that a small company of actors from New York City would be performing both on the ice and later that evening on stage inside the grand resort.

The crowd roared with a robust cheer that echoed off the surrounding mountains. The performer bowed graciously to the audience as he skated to the edge of the pond. His cheeks were rosy from the cold, but his face was covered with a sheen of perspiration. Slowly, the crowd began to thin as people moved back toward the resort.

"He was rather entertaining," an older woman commented as she linked arms with a beautiful, dark-haired woman.

"I thought that he looked rather silly, myself," a rosy-cheeked man said as he led the· women carefully back to the resort.

"Oh, pish," the older woman scolded. "You've never liked that sort of thing, anyway. You'll find the play scheduled this evening and some vaudeville acts after that more to your fancy, dear. Eliza, would you care to join your father and me for the play? I have been told that it caused quite a commotion on Broadway."

Eliza felt her heart flutter. She knew that Alex was in the hotel somewhere, though she hadn't seen him since she arrived three days prior. He was the only reason she had agreed to go with her parents on leave while her husband was away on extended business. Though Eliza had tried to forget him, she found her thoughts turning to Alex at odd hours of the day. She nodded, but said nothing as they stepped into the warmth of the resort.

Eliza's thoughts returned to the kiss she had shared with the Irish actor on the stage. She blushed despite the darkness the enveloped the audience. Although she had told herself that nothing would ever happen between her and Alex, her emotions betrayed her resolve. Before she knew it, a plan had formed in her mind. She swore to herself that if it didn't work, she would simply go home to her husband and forget she ever knew Alex.

It was late by the time that the final vaudeville performer left the stage and the house lights came on. Eliza rose from her seat and clung to her father's arm as the crowds exited. Eliza bid her parents good night at the door to her suite. She undressed and slid into a white silk gown that touched the floor. In front of the mirror, she removed her cosmetics and brushed her long wavy black hair until it shone in the lamplight. Periodically, she checked the time as she moved slowly at her tasks.

Eliza waited until the resort fell into a deep silence and the hall lights were dimmed for the evening. It was nearing one-thirty in the morning when she pulled the door to her suite open and peered into the hallway. If she was going to do what she had planned, it would mean descending two floors in her night attire and moving silently down a long hallway to the rooms where the performers slept. She had slyly acquired the information she needed from a room attendant, including where Alex slept.

"If I do not move now, I shall not dare to move at all," she told herself as she placed one foot over the threshold. She moved swiftly and silently down the hall to the staircase. The heavy, thick carpeting swallowed up the sounds of her steps. Eliza briskly moved down the hallway until she stood outside Alex's suite. She tried the handle and found it unlocked. She slid into the room and silently secured the door. When her eyes adjusted to the darkness, she moved carefully to the bedroom door.

Eliza paused for a moment at the foot of the bed and watched Alex sleeping. He looked so young and innocent in the bath of moonlight that filled the room. Her heart pounded. Something stirred within her, and her voice reflected a husky tone when she called his name.

Alex stirred in his bed and awakened when Eliza spoke his name the second time. In the moonlight, Alex blinked the sleep out of his eyes as he reached for the oil lamp by his bed. "Eliza?" Alex asked sleepily as he touched the match to the wick. When he turned his eyes back to the figure standing at the foot of his bed, he saw Eliza unbuttoning the front of her gown.

"What in God's name are you doing here, child?" he asked as he pushed the blankets away from him and rose from the bed.

Eliza smiled, "I'm not a child."

Alex rose from the bed and stayed Eliza's hand as she worked at a stubborn button on her gown. He was trembling. "Don't, I pray you," Alex said, holding Eliza's hand still.

"Alex, please listen to me," Eliza pleaded. "I can't seem to clear my mind of you. The memory of your touch burns through me at night when I lie awake in the stillness. No one has ever stirred in me what you have. I love you." Tears touched her pleading eyes. She could feel Alex's hand as it tensed on her own.

"Oh, God, girl, you don't know what you're saying." Alex gritted his teeth to disguise the passion that colored his voice.

Eliza's eyes flashed anger, "Do you care for me at all, Alex?"

He nodded slowly, "That I do."

Eliza moved his hand inside of her open gown and pressed it to her breast. "Make love to me."

Alex retreated across the room as though he had been burned. With his face to the window he said softly,

"I can't, Eliza. You simply don't understand." His hand, shaking, ran through the stock of short red hair on his head. He offered nothing more.

"Then make me understand," Eliza said, moving to the window where Alex stood.

"I am a woman," Alex offered as tears streaked her face.

Eliza felt as though she had been struck by lightning. Her mind reeled. In all of her sheltered life she had never heard of such things. She was in love with a woman who pretended to be a man! She wondered if she was possessed by a demon as Monsignor Pushkin had talked about in one of his fiery sermons. No. Whatever had hold of her certainly wasn't natural. Or was it? Her thoughts bantered back and forth. One thing she knew. Being with her husband was the most *un*natural thing she had ever done.

"I'm sorry," Alex said turning her face from the window, "I didn't mean to hurt you. I tried to keep you away."

Eliza felt betrayed by her own thoughts. Alex's touch still burned on her breast. A shiver ran through her body, and her body tingled in ways she hadn't known were possible. She turned and ran from the room. She needed time to think and to reason out all of the feelings that clouded her mind.

For two days, Eliza kept her own company until her mother insisted that a doctor see her. Eliza shook her head. She rose from her bed, claiming that she felt much better. The following evening, at the majestic ball on their final night at the resort, Eliza appeared to be her normal self.

Eliza danced with her father and with other gentlemen who knew her husband. It wasn't until the end of the night that she saw Alex. Alex, dressed in formal men's attire, led a young woman to the large dance floor. Eliza watched with wonder as Alex led the girl gracefully in the dance. The feelings that she had so carefully buried sprang to the surface. Her heart pounded.

Her mother placed a caring hand on her elbow, but Eliza waved off her concern. "I'm all right, Mom Ma," she said watching the couple dance. Her mother followed her gaze, and it was then that she knew what had ailed her child.

"An actor, child?" Concern etched her face.

Eliza smiled, "No, Mom Ma, it is nothing to concern yourself with."

Her mother's eyes scrutinized her, looking for some sort of truth. She had known for some time that Eliza wasn't happy in her marriage, even though her husband seemed to treat her well. The Wittacker line and fortune went back for many generations, and the match was a good one. She had hoped that Eliza could learn to love the man over the years.

Eliza heard her mother sigh and knew that more questions were forthcoming. She was relieved when her father held out his hand, and her mother had no choice but to join him in the next dance.

When Eliza turned her attention back to the dance floor, she could not see Alex anywhere among the couples that milled around preparing for the next dance. She opened her fan and waved it in front of her. It was almost too warm to bear. She closed her eyes to enjoy the breeze on her face. She was startled by a voice very near her.

"May I ask you to dance?" Alex said, holding out her hand. Eliza was surprised, but she held out her hand. Alex smiled as she led Eliza to their position on the floor. With one hand on Eliza's waist and the other holding her hand out, Alex began to lead her when the refrains of Mozart filled the air.

At first Eliza would not look into her eyes, though Alex could not keep from staring at her. Finally, Eliza couldn't look away. She allowed her eyes to wander over Alex's face before she looked into her eyes. "I should have known," Eliza began as she gathered her scattered thoughts together. "The smooth face and delicate features. I should have known." Alex smiled softly but said nothing. "Is your name really Alex?" Eliza asked. "Or is that fake, too?"

"I'm not a fake, Eliza, I did what I had to do to keep off the streets with my brother. My name is Alexandria O'Connor, and I came here when I was younger with my parents from Ireland," Alex said as she skillfully danced Eliza across the floor. "My company is leaving tomorrow. We're going back to New York City. I would wish to see you again before I go, if you choose," Alex said shyly as the dance ended.

Eliza curtsied briskly, "Suite 513."

Alex waited until she could stand to look at the wintry scene outside her window no longer. She stepped into the hallway, nodded her head slightly to a gentleman, and tipped her hat to his lady companion before she moved down the hall. Outside Eliza's door, Alex tapped gently. She knew the woman's parents were sleeping right across the hall. The door opened slightly and then all the way. Alex slipped inside, but not before another woman, who had watched Alex and Eliza all night with envious eyes, saw her enter.

Eliza was dressed for the night in a soft blue dressing gown made of silk. Alex could feel her heart beat against her chest. Before she could stop the words, she said, "You look so beautiful." A faint smile touched Eliza's lips. She didn't know why she had invited Alex to her room.

Eliza moved across the sitting room and opened the cabinet where her husband kept his whiskey. "Would you care for a taste?" she asked, holding up a crystal decanter. Alex shook her head. Eliza shrugged and smiled, "I should think that I need one." She had never taken a drink in her life, and the taste made her gag. She coughed as the amber liquid burned in her stomach.

"Eliza," Alex began as she moved across the room. She took the cup from Eliza's hand. "I fear I will never see you again after tonight."

Alex touched Eliza's hair, which shimmered in the light of the oil lamps. It was soft in Alex's hand. A gentle, rosewater scent filled her senses and intoxicated her with desire. She touched Eliza's face with the back of her hand. Her body awakened to new desires, and the second kiss was sweeter than the first. As Alex pulled her tighter, Eliza's knees gave way under her. In one fluid motion, Alex picked her up in her arms and carried her into the dark bedroom beyond.

No words needed to be said as Alex unbuttoned the front of Eliza's gown. With patient and gentle hands, she touched Eliza's soft skin as the gown fell to the floor. She followed the line of Eliza's neck with her lips while her hands moved along the soft curves of her hips and came to rest on her buttocks.

Eliza opened the front of her shirt, and Alex felt her body respond. Eliza's long fingers shyly touched Alex. Starting with her face, Eliza moved down her neck to her shoulders and came to rest on her breast. She caressed the delicate curves of Alex's breast until her nipple stood taut and aroused. In all her life, Eliza had never touched anything so wondrous. All the while, Eliza looked into the eyes of her lover, which were clouded with passion.

Alex allowed her shirt to fall. Eliza parted her lips as a wave of passion swept over her. Alex moved her gently to the bed. Eliza felt her passion rise as Alex came to rest beside her. Alex kissed her deeply and shifted her leg across Eliza's thigh until it came to rest between her legs.

Eliza fumbled with the buttons of her lover's pants and Alex lifted her hips slightly to allow Eliza to slide them off. In the still moonlight, Eliza admired the body that lay next to her. She caressed Alex's silky skin; Alex moaned and whispered Eliza's name.

Alex pushed her body up and shifted herself until she was above Eliza. Eliza stretched out her legs to let her lover in and entwined her fingers in Alex's hair. Alex ran her tongue along the lobe of Eliza's ear. Eliza felt the silky warmth of Alex's body as she pressed into her. Passion exploded from Eliza's body. She followed Alex's motion as she pressed her hands into the small of Alex's back. Their mouths joined and Eliza parted her lips, welcoming Alex inside.

Eliza moaned with pleasure as Alex burned a trail across her skin to her breast. Alex whispered softly against her skin as her tongue set Eliza's breast aflame.

Eliza pushed Alex onto her back and freely explored

the smoothness of Alex's skin from her breast to the flat of Alex's stomach. Exhilaration filled her senses as she moved her fingers between Alex's legs. She lingered there before she dared to touch the place of her lover's desire and heated passion. Alex's body quivered as a moan escaped her throat.

Bethany O'Connor awoke with a start. The tiny bedroom of her shack was bathed in moonlight. She could hear Keva breathing in the dark shadows. It took her a moment to orient herself to what had caused her to waken so abruptly.

She listened. Silence. *What is it?* Nothing came to her as she lay in the darkness.

She pulled the blanket up to her chin, though the night was very warm. Something had disturbed her from within, and it was still calling to her from the blackness of the forest beyond. It was the same thing she had felt when the Michaels had moved to the property beyond her own. But this time the impression was stronger.

Slowly she began to pull into herself. She trained her conscious mind on one thought and focused her energy where her heart pounded in her chest. Soon she heard nothing but her own mental voice. In a rush, like a strong wind, and with a flash of light, Bethany stood next to her body. She gazed down at the sleeping figure for a moment. This was not new to her, she had traveled this way many times in the past.

Bethany glanced to the open window of her room and moved there with a simple thought. Keva snorted and rose to her feet. Bethany spoke in thought to the bear, who understood and lay protectively near the woman's body. Bethany moved beyond the window and into the night.

Bethany relished the sight of the moon. Though her physical body was blind, her astral body could distinguish all things in her environment. Bethany O'Connor moved rapidly, a bird in flight. The inky blackness that she knew to be evil invaded her senses with each foot closer she dared travel toward it.

At first Emily listened skeptically to the words that Jackie put to her. It seemed an outrageous story even to a woman who believed in the supernatural. "Okay, now wait a minute, you're telling me that Christine was told to commit suicide by a coven of black witches who live around here because she had seen something that she wasn't supposed to. And, you're telling me that Danielle had something to do with that. Now, come on, how stupid do you think I am?"

Jackie looked hurt. "I'm telling you the truth because I thought you were the most open to what I had to say. I know it sounds farfetched, but I'm telling the truth. I swear."

Emily raised her hand. "Suppose you tell me how they managed to do this."

Jackie smiled. "Easy. They hexed her."

"Get out of town," Emily said laughing.

"What's the matter? You don't believe in such things? You, a woman who makes a living telling other people's fortunes, don't believe in witches and hexes and all of that? I'm surprised, Emily." Jackie was telling the truth as best she could, but she was deleting and adding information here and there to keep the game alive. She didn't want to spill all her cards. She knew there was a small chance that Emily might remember this conversation tomorrow.

"You know what I wonder, Emily?" Jackie said as the two stopped in a patch of moonlight that broke through the forest.

Emily looked the girl in the eye. "I'm dying to find out. What?"

Jackie's eyes were alluring, and Emily found she could not break from the stare. "I know who you are now," Jackie said. "I know everything there is to know about you and your sad little life back in Portland, but I wonder who you are underneath it all." Jackie used her words carefully as her mind pulled at the fringes of Emily's.

Emily found herself fighting to regain control as she looked into Jackie's eyes. Soon, the only thing that she could see was the deep blackness of the pupils.

Jackie continued unhurried. "I wonder who you'll be when you come out of the night and stand naked before the Creator of all things. Naked as we all must go before that divine one. Oh, yes, Emily I can see it in your eyes. You try so feebly not to believe in the wondrous being that most call God, and that's your weakness. It surrounds you like a cheap and petty robe."

Emily heard the words as they came into her mind. She wanted to pull away. She wanted to run, but her limbs were frozen in place. She could hear her own thoughts as they screamed to be released.

How did she know about that? Emily thought in fear. She had never shared her struggle with her faith with anyone, yet this girl seemed to be able to probe her soul.

"Open up and let me in, Emily. Show me who you'll be when you stand before Him, I implore you. Can you hear His voice calling to you from far off. 'Join me,' he says. 'Join me, Emily.' " Jackie sensed Emily weakening. She was almost there. She had never gotten so close to someone's soul before, and it gave her an incredible feeling of power.

"Cease this at once," a voice commanded from somewhere in the blackness. Jackie turned. She was startled to see a figure standing four yards to her right. A dim light surrounded the naked body of the woman. Her long, silver hair flowed in a breeze of its own, and her face was young and beautiful. Jackie was stunned. She wasn't sure who the woman was, but she had never seen anyone like her before. She tried mentally to explore the woman's mind, but she only got a glimpse before it slammed shut like a steel door.

Jackie turned to Emily. "Leave this place and forget anything ever happened here tonight," she commanded before she fled from the strange woman whose feet floated a few inches from the ground.

Over her shoulder, Jackie yelled a warning. "Don't fuck with us, bitch, or you'll die."

TEN

Ashley pulled away from the vision as it faded into the blackness of her mind. She could still feel the passion between the two women that filled the room. As she opened her eyes, she heard Catherine clearing her throat.

"Well, that was interesting. Thank you, dear," Patricia said, rising quickly from the floor.

Olivia rose at the same time. "I should say," she commented as she pushed her clothes back into place.

Ashley shrugged, "Hey, it's not my fault. I told you that I saw it so fast that I couldn't decipher what it was. Besides, now we know something about the people who died in that mine." Catherine nodded, but she didn't trust her voice to say anything.

Patricia glanced at her watch. She was alarmed to find that they had spent almost two hours in the vision. Her thoughts turned toward Emily. Something was wrong. "I think that we should start worrying about Emily. She's not back yet. You did leave her a note, didn't you dear?" Patricia asked.

Ashley nodded as she rose and stretched her muscles. It was odd even for Emily to be gone so long. "Guess we'd better go look for her," Ashley said as she moved to the door.

Olivia looked alarmed, "You don't think anything happened to her out there, do you?"

Patricia thought for a moment. She shrugged, "I can't tell, but I think she might be in danger."

Emily woke standing on her feet. She could hear the voices of her friends from far away, and she opened her mouth to respond. Her thoughts were far away and vague. She closed her mouth without saying a word. Her body felt like lead. She was puzzled. She tried to decipher her thoughts and organize them in some fashion.

The friends' voices were closer, and this time when she opened her mouth she was able to squeak out one word. "Help," Emily called into the night. She trembled with fear as the inky blackness seemed to close around her.

"I think she's over here." Within a dozen strides, Ashley was by her side. Ashley took Emily into her arms and scolded, "Where in the hell have you been? And what the hell have you been doing? Do you realize that it's after midnight?" Ashley saw the vacant look in her friend's eyes and felt a cold chill creep down her spine.

Within a few minutes, Patricia and Catherine had caught up. Both women held their tongues when they saw Emily's face in the half moonlight. The women quickly escorted Emily to the house where Olivia was waiting for them with hot cups of coffee. Emily looked pale in the light of the dining room when her friends led her to a chair.

Amanda entered with a shotgun in her hands. She placed the gun on the table as a look of concern stitched across her face. She had feared the worst since Emily had been missing since seven-thirty that evening. "Thank God, you found her," was all she could say as she pulled a chair out and sat heavily in it. She watched Emily from across the table and wondered.

Amanda had seen Emily and Jackie move off into the wooded area of the immense property and had thought about calling to them to warn them not to wander too far off. Jackie knew the woods, though, and Amanda disregarded the feeling of foreboding that hung over her.

Jackie didn't know it, but when she couldn't sleep and stared out the window of her room, Amanda had seen Jackie sneaking out late at night. She had not mentioned the late-night escapades to anyone. She figured that the girl needed some time to clear her head. Amanda knew about Jackie's life before she had come here, and she thought that Jackie just needed some time and space to think through her problems. Amanda had often wondered what it would have been like if she, too, had been abandoned by her parents, but the feelings were quickly shoved off.

As Amanda rubbed her finger across her upper lip and watched Emily from across the table, she wondered why Jackie had left her there in the darkness alone. She made a mental note to talk to Jackie tomorrow. She would have a good explanation.

Ashley rubbed Emily's back and looked at her with a pinched expression of worry. Emily just stared with blank eyes at the tablecloth. She did not respond at all to their questions. Not even her eyes gave a clue.

At Patricia's suggestion, Ashley led Emily upstairs to her room, undressed her, and put her to bed. As Ashley stared down at her friend, a hundred thoughts ran through her mind. Ashley was about to pose another question when Emily spoke.

"I'm okay. I'm just tired, so very tired," Emily said, closing her eyes and rolling onto her side away from Ashley.

"Okay, baby," Ashley said softly. "You just rest now." She looked over her shoulder one last time before she turned out the light and closed the door.

Patricia pulled the sheet up to her chin and settled into bed. With the pillows propped up behind her head, she opened the tome that she and Emily had brought with them. The pages were old and yellow but seemed to have withstood the damage of the years.

She moved through the pages one at a time with

the fascination of a child searching for some elusive answer that would not come to her. There were sketches of witches dating back to the eighteenth century. On opposite pages, across from the sketches, were profiles of the individuals. Some profiles went the length of one page, while others occupied up to a dozen pages.

She wasn't sure what she was looking for, other than the name *O'Connor,* which stuck in her mind. She had thumbed through more than three quarters of the book when the face of a man stopped her. His features were hard and cold, as though someone had chiseled them from a piece of granite. The photograph was old and faded, but Patricia could see his eyes clearly. A chill ran though her. She felt if she looked at the photo for any length of time those eyes would bore into her soul. She reminded herself that the photo was a still glimpse into the past and was not a living thing. But, her mind argued, the eyes seem so real.

Ashley lay awake in the darkness and listened to Catherine as she slept in her arms. Her mind kept playing over Emily's face. For almost an hour, Ashley had tried to analyze what had happened to her friend. She had known Emily for a good part of her life and had never known her to be without words. Her only conclusion was that something had frightened Emily terriblly out there. She had no clue what it was. She could only hope that Emily would be better tomorrow. *Maybe Teri will have more influence on her,* Ashley thought as she remembered her telephone conversation with her earlier in the evening. Teri had said that she would be at the school sometime tomorrow in the late afternoon.

Ashley allowed her mind to chase around the endless possibilities of what happened until she rose from her bed and sat at the window. She knew that she would eventually have to let it go until they could get some answers from Emily. At least she didn't look like she had received any physical trauma.

Perhaps she's been hexed, Ashley thought. She restrained herself from laughing at the absurd idea. "That is the craziest thing I have ever heard of," she scolded herself in the darkness. She repeatedly tried to shove the idea to the back of her mind until she gave in and looked at it. *What is witchcraft exactly, and how do hexes work?* she puzzled. She tried hard to remember what she had read on the subject. It took a while to recall the facts.

As with everything in the realm of the supernatural, there were two schools of study other than that of neutrality. There were those who believed in the possibility of witchcraft and those who did not. Ashley tended toward the idea that it did not exist, but she called to mind the books that spoke of the truest nature of the craft.

Witches could practice in covens of as little as three people or as large as twenty, but the ideal number was thirteen. A High Priest or Priestess leads the others in worship of their deity. She remembered something about a Horned God. Everything seemed jumbled as she tried to recall all that she had read. She could not recollect anything about hexes, curses, or spells.

Bethany O'Connor came to her mind. Emily and

Patricia had tried to see the woman earlier in the day without any luck. Ashley wondered if she would know anything more than they collectively knew about witchcraft. If she did, Ashley wondered, would she be willing to share what she knew about it? Ashley was convinced that they were drawing closer to what was really going on at the school and that what happened to Emily was a warning of what was to come if they stayed.

Bethany O'Connor felt very weak as she slipped back into her body. She fought sleep and rose on her elbows. Keva's large head loomed above her in the still blackness. She grunted and moved her large body to the foot of the bed where she sat, watching Bethany.

Bethany struggled to rise. A half dozen thoughts ran through her mind at once. Each thought tried to prevail over the other as she sought to gain control over them.

Finally, she came to her feet. She reached for her walking stick to help her feel her way through the cabin. From one of many bookshelves that lined the front room, she found a large tome. Bethany carried the heavy, thick book to the small kitchen table and opened it. She knew by touch the exact page she was seeking. It had taken her many years to compile her mother's book into Braille and yet another many years to add her own knowledge, wisdom, and beliefs.

Her fingers working quickly, Bethany searched the pages. Time worked against her. She had a precious few days to regain the power and knowledge to do what should have been done years ago. Her only hope was that it was not too late already.

Jackie waited until the only sounds that filled the room were those of Stephanie as she slept. As quickly and quietly as she could, Jackie slipped out of her bed and opened the window. She climbed out on the roof, just as she had done many times in the past. Jackie quickly scanned the ground that lay in blackness beyond the floodlights. She knew someone would be waiting for her as usual.

In haste, a figure slipped out of the night and placed a ladder against the lowest point of the roof. Jackie carefully climbed down the overhangs until she reached it.

Once on the ground, she was greeted simply by silence as the figure pulled the ladder away and slipped into the blackness. Jackie followed without a word. She pulled on her long, black robe as she melted into the forest beyond. She was unaware that someone watched her from one of the many darkened windows of the school.

ELEVEN

The High Priestess drew herself to her feet before the waiting people of the coven. Her face was obscured by the black hood she wore over her head. No one in the coven knew who she was, and she kept it that way. She was the High Priestess, and that was all they needed to know.

It was time to form the circle. It was time to worship the Horned God. It was time to fly with the magic of the universe. This would be the last meeting before tomorrow night when they would gather for one final time. Through the powers of her magic and the will of the coven, the portal of time would open and the past would be changed. Her heart raced with the thoughts of revenge, power, and riches.

Tomorrow night the dark mine would yield all, and God help anyone who stood in her way. By this time tomorrow, Olivia would be dead, and her daughter's blood would be the sacrifice necessary to tear the fabric of time. *Amanda will pay for the blood of the coven she spilled.* Not even Bethany O'Connor, with her weak powers and half-dead spells, could stop her now. It was too late. The plan had been laid out too carefully for her to interfere with it.

The High Priestess raised her hooded head and laughed at the stars that twinkled down on the coven. The echo of her laughter reached above the treetops and dared to disturb even God in his dreamlike sleep somewhere in the universe.

Bethany O'Connor felt the chill hand of fate. Her eyes, which saw only blackness, suddenly were filled with a vision.

Blood was splashed across the stones in front of the mine behind the school. People moved in the blackness as if they *were* the very blackness. A chant rose through the air, beginning softly, barely disturbing the night air, before working into a crescendo.

A pulsating electrical energy filled the night. Each time the energy would rise to another high, fade back a bit, and then rise even more in power. Bethany could not understand what was happening.

Bethany felt the universe pull and contract around her. It seemed to shrink away, somehow change. What was happening to the universe was happening to her as well.

What is happening here? Bethany cried out in her thoughts. She felt insignificant and powerless to change anything. She felt a tugging in the deepest part of her mind. Someone was with her, a welcome trespasser who had melded with her on the same psychic wavelength. It was the woman she had seen when she dream-walked earlier. *Emily.* She called her by name but heard no answer. The existence of time warbled and faded, bounced back, and warbled again. *What is happening here?* Bethany again called to Emily.

This time she heard an answer from far away, but the words faded before they reached her. Summoning all her powers, Bethany challenged the vision and moved closer to the people at the mouth of the mine. There, Bethany saw who challenged the universe. As she attempted to move closer to the hooded figure, it was like swimming through jelly. In one hand the figure held a black-handled knife. As Bethany drew agonizingly closer, she recognized the knife as an athame, the core of the figure's power.

An inch at a time Bethany moved her hand out of the gelatinous void. She reached for the hood of the figure and, in a last burst of energy, snapped off the hood.

"Enough," the woman beneath the hood called angrily into the night.

Bethany was snapped, like an object in a taut rubber band, back to the present. A fine sheen of sweat covered her body and dampened her hair. She rose on trembling legs. With her hand on Keva's great neck, she found her way to the door that would lead her into the night.

* * * * *

The High Priestess raised her head before the coven. Hidden within the deep folds of the hood, her face was pinched and drawn. She had showed too much. She had wished to gloat a bit to the one woman who would understand what was to happen on August Eve, but she had never intended the other person she knew as Emily to come in the way that she had. Her mind worked hard at a furious pace as she tried to figure out what her next move should be.

She thought of the conversation she had with Jackie earlier. Perhaps the hex that Jackie had put on Emily was not enough to keep her away. Though Jackie was strong, she was still a new member in the coven and had not learned enough to do something so vital for the plan to work. At best, the woman had hoped that Emily could be persuaded to join the coven in one way or another. At the very worst, she had hoped that the suggestion of fear that Jackie had planted would be enough to drive the woman and her friends back to Oregon. It now appeared that neither would be true. And now, Emily knew too much, as did Bethany O'Connor.

The High Priestess puzzled over the new development. Something would have to be done before tomorrow. She was no stranger to murder. After all, she had planned and executed one already. Another two people would die at her hand tomorrow.

She sighed. It had not been in her plan, but the other women would have to die, too. All of them, including Bethany, would be dead before tomorrow night.

The followers passed the black candles around silently. Each one knew what this meant, and they served without question. From the central candle that burned where the High Priestess stood, one of the robed figures lit her candle. She was second only to the priestess. Each woman lit her candle in succession until the circle was illuminated fully.

The High Priestess opened the Book of Shadows to the appropriate page. When she spoke, her words were in an ancient language far older than the language of the early churches. She spoke in a language that only the Horned God could understand fully, which she sometimes shared with her most precious followers. The High Priestess understood the words that she spoke this night. The words were translated in her mind as she spoke.

"Come death, ancient and cold. Come from the five corners of the universe that shall be lifted up for your passing by the Horned God." With this the High Priestess raised her athame with the blade pointing to the ground and her arms pointing straight out in front of her at the five points of the universe. A slight breeze moved her black robe. The wind touched only her robe, not the others. The woman shivered, but a smile played across her lips.

The rest of the robed people had knelt when the Book of Shadows was opened, and now they chanted the words that the priestess said, though none of them knew what they meant.

"Come death, I command you, servant of the Horned God. Come now and hear my voice. Visit now, ancient one, in this hour of darkness, my enemies that wish to prevail over me. Visit them, each one, and steal their life from them. Their souls shall be your reward." The woman grazed her wrist with the sharp blade of the athame and allowed her own blood to flow into a silver-hued cup. The blood ran until the wound sealed itself. "As an offering of the covenant that I have made with the Horned God, I offer you this as sacrifice." She held the cup away from her in the same manner as before and pointed to the five points of the universe. There was a tingling sensation in her hands.

When she lowered the cup to the rock in front of her, all but a fifth of the blood was gone from the cup. With skilled hands, the woman opened a pouch and pulled out small glass vials that contained different herbs. She measured a tiny portion from each and sprinkled the herbs into the cup. With the athame, she stirred the concoction. The woman brought the cup to her lips and swallowed the brew in one sip.

To the High Priestess's eyes alone, death appeared, standing before her. She swooned and threatened the edges of her consciousness. She fought to control herself.

A black cloud swirled around her body and absorbed her energy. Death was preparing itself for the slaughter that lay ahead. For a single moment, she could feel the marvelously evil joy that was projected from the cloud. She fought her fear and remained strong. She had lived through this before, and she would live through it again until the time came to fulfill the pact that she had made. She pushed all thoughts from her mind as the cloud swirled around faster and faster. Soon, it would be time.

* * * * *

Emily woke with a start. Her eyes snapped open. Her bed sheets were soaked with perspiration. At first she didn't know where she was. But as her eyes scanned the darkness, the dream came back to her. Nausea rose in her throat. Two voices fought for attention. The one voice she recognized as her own, but the other seemed distant and unfamiliar. The sound of the voice caused fear to knot in her stomach and rise up her throat. She could not think on her own or see inside the dream without the fear and nausea attacking her.

Emily rose from her bed and rested at the window seat. Far off in the distance a small fire burned in the night. Tears burned her eyes as she fought to read her own thoughts that blurred in and out of focus.

Emily began with the easy stuff. She knew who she was and where she was. She knew why she was here. She knew all the common things about herself and her friends.

As she moved on to what had happened earlier in the evening, she saw a face loom in front of her. She tried to put a name to the face. *Jackie,* she thought. The fear got tighter in her belly. She stopped her mind for a moment and allowed her shoulders to relax.

Emily's head pounded. With determination, she struggled to take another step into her mind. She had gone out into the night to get a breath of air and figure out where the investigation was going. She remembered that with ease, though the nausea threatened to overtake her. Emily moved on and on through her memory until it played out before her in a gush of fear and a wave of nausea. She held firm until the end.

Carefully, Emily sorted back through it all. Her thoughts slowly became her own again. Jackie's will was strong, and the bond seemed to be impenetrable. Emily wasn't sure what Jackie had done to her, but she knew one thing for certain. When Jackie intruded into her thoughts and left the suggestion there, she had also left a residue of her own thoughts and fears behind. Emily concentrated on those now. Somewhere in all of it, Emily knew that she could find what she sought. The answers to the questions ran through her mind, some clues to the investigation. With this information, and the revelations that the vision had shown, Emily knew that she might possibly have enough to end the nightmare that had haunted the Michaels for years.

TWELVE

Bethany moved through the black forest with the precision of a sighted woman. She had covered the path may times before with the help of Keva. The next few steps would bring her to the front door of the school. Her grip tightened on the leather pouch that she carried.

She could feel a sticky sort of coolness that clung to her body in the night air. She smelled the wind that blew from the east. The hair prickled on the back of her neck and on her arms. With renewed determination, she quickened her step until she was standing on the front porch. She would only have a few minutes to wake the household.

Olivia heard pounding. The distant sound came closer to her with the seconds that slid away. She could hear a man's voice in the void.

"Tickets, please," he called as the knocking got closer. Olivia opened her eyes and found herself swaying on a train in a seat next to Alex O'Connor. The two were so close that their shoulders almost touched, but Alex seemed not to see her as she stared out the window at the landscape passing before them.

Alex was dressed like a man with a full face of whiskers. Across from her was a boy and the woman Eliza. Eliza rested her head on the cushioned back of the seat while the boy slept against her. Alex was writing in a diary. Her brows were knit in concentration and anger.

When the conductor came to the door of their cabin, Alex laid the pen and journal aside on what should have been Olivia's lap. Olivia gasped as she looked through herself to the open page. At first, her mind registered the absolute impossibility of this happening. Then she remembered the advice Patricia had given her, and Olivia relaxed enough to read the words on the page.

The words were written in the flowing, loose hand of someone whose thoughts run faster than the pen. It was hard to read, and Olivia had to read through the sentences twice before they made sense to her.

How can I tell Eliza that he knows about me? How can I tell her that he knows about us and how twisted this all seems to be in my head right now. I know of the teachings of the church. I know what they say about people who live lies and who love the wrong people. But I don't care if my mortal soul is in danger. I love her.

Suddenly the diary was moved as Alex returned to the seat. She poised the pen above the page as her thoughts began to flow again. Olivia sensed herself drifting to somewhere that her physical body could not possibly go. She relaxed and allowed it to happen. Looking over Alex's left shoulder, Olivia read the words that followed.

I am ashamed that I have dragged her into this insanity. I should not have come that night. I should have kept my peace at my residence and let well enough alone, but I didn't.

Eliza has to know. Soon, I will begin to show the signs of the life that grows within me. I am afraid, and I pray that the Goddess will keep me strong. When I tell her I will have to tell her how this came to be. What do I say then? That her husband took me by force. That I fought him and scarred his face with my knife. That he won over me. And that is why I had to run.

Oh, Goddess, hear me now. I never meant to harm anyone. I never asked for Eliza to follow me. But what do I do now? He will follow us, and some day he will find us just as his black witchcraft found out about me.

His heart is black and the evil that he conjures chills my soul. I have seen the power of his evil as he threatened me that night with a death that would take days to accomplish. I still bear the brand that he put on me that night on the inside of my thigh.

What will I tell her? So pure is she as she sleeps there in front of me. Her heart is surely made of the finest glass. It would shatter her to know the truth.

From across the cabin of the train, Eliza stirred and her eyes fluttered open. A smile touched her lips as she gazed across at her lover. She would be glad when Alex no longer wore the disguise. She reached her hand across the distance. Alex touched the softness of her hand with her own. A trembling smile played across her lips.

Ashley woke Catherine when she heard the pounding at the front door. The women opened their bedroom door and peered out into the hallway. Patricia was there already, with her reading glasses still propped on her nose where they had been when she fell asleep a few hours before. Emily was just coming out of her room. No one from the apartment on the next floor stirred.

"What in the hell is that racket?" Ashley asked, breaking the silence. Patricia shrugged as Emily came up behind her.

"May I suggest that we go find out before the whole place comes down around our ears?" Catherine asked as she moved down the hallway. Patricia followed closely behind, with Ashley and Emily in tow.

Bethany heard one of the doors squeak open. She could not see the four wild-eyed women who gazed out into the darkness at her. She sensed their fear and said reassuringly, "My name is Bethany O'Connor. Please, it is important that I speak to you right away."

She sensed the door widening a little until Keva gave a snort and someone gasped out of fear.

Bethany stepped forward. "It's all right," she assured them, holding out her hands. "She is my friend. Please, I don't have much time."

"What do you want?" a voice asked slightly to the left of her.

Bethany opened the leather pouch and pulled out four crystals from it. She thrust them into her open palm. "Take one, each of you." It was a command rather than a request.

There was a moment of hesitation. "Look over my shoulder toward where the sun will be rising soon in the sky. What do you see?" Bethany asked, though she knew what was coming. She could smell the stale stench as it rode just behind her all the way to the school.

Ashley saw it first. It was blacker than the night that tried to conceal it. A thick, black cloud twisted and bent its shape at will. First it was a black horse thundering through the sky; then it shaped itself into a hideous creature unlike any the earth had ever seen. An evil wind rose as a premonition before the cloud, and it smelled of dead things hidden away in the bowels of hell. The women stood frozen to their spots as the thing approached.

Patricia muttered, "Oh, God, just make it go away. I swear I will never read another book on demonology again."

Catherine instinctively grabbed for the cross at her throat.

"Take them now, damn it," Bethany ordered. This seemed to break the trance of the women. Each grabbed a light blue crystal from her hand.

The crystal seemed to take on a life of its own in

Ashley's hand as it glowed ever so slightly. She pulled her eyes away from the crystal in time to see the specter closing in within a few hundred yards.

The thing formed a funnel cloud and came down on all the women. It swirled around in a fury. Ashley clutched the crystal to her heart and closed her eyes. She could feel the thing pulling at her, trying to figure out a way into her body. Somewhere in the confusion she heard Bethany O'Connor shouting something that sounded like a chant.

As quickly as the thing descended from the air, it was gone. With a sound of rushing water and a piercing cry of fury, the black cloud dissipated into the night that had spawned it.

When Ashley dared to open her eyes again, she discovered that Bethany and the bear had disappeared into the night as well. She opened her hand and peered at the crystal. The glow that she thought she had seen before was gone. It was simply a light blue crystal with a design carved into it.

Ashley fought the urge to laugh when she caught a glimpse of her mother. The wind that had assailed them had twirled her mother's long red hair into a bizarre sort of beehive. It was standing straight up in the air.

"And what is so amusing?" Ashley asked Catherine who was chuckling beside her.

"Ashley, your hair is standing straight up on your head," Catherine said, reaching to touch the other's hair.

"Well, I wouldn't laugh so hard, yours is doing the same thing," Ashley challenged.

"I think that we had better go in," Emily said from behind.

The women self-consciously pushed their hair down as they walked into the school. Emily checked the doors twice to assure herself that they were safely locked in.

"That thing. Everybody saw it, right?" Emily asked as she joined the others at the kitchen table. When they all nodded she went on, "I don't think that we should go anywhere from now on without these crystals, just in case it comes back."

"Anybody have any ideas what that thing was out there?" Ashley asked.

Patricia shrugged, "I thought it was a demon or something."

"Well, one thing is for certain," Emily said as she tiredly pulled a chair out and sat in it. "The thing was charged with so much static electricity that it made our hair stand up. I could hear it cracking and popping as it circled us."

Ashley smiled, "That theory surprises me, coming from you. I thought you would be more in line with Mother's thoughts."

Emily shrugged, "I didn't say that it wasn't a demon or something of that nature. I was only making an observation."

Catherine shivered, "One time when I was in the convent, I had the opportunity to see an exorcism."

Patricia cut her off. "I thought that the church no longer did such barbaric things."

Catherine shrugged, "That's what they tell the lay people. They think that most common folk would not be able to handle the real truth as the church sees it."

"It's a good thing that I'm not Catholic. Otherwise, that might tend to piss me off a bit," said Ashley.

Catherine ignored her. "Anyway, it was moments after the exorcism began that I swear to this day that I saw something looming just above the body of the person who was possessed. It was as black as tar and shaped in the form of a cloud. It changed shapes in front of me. No one else saw it, so I kept my mouth shut. I left there a week later with some other sisters when we returned to the motherhouse."

"So what you're saying is that we all saw a demon of some sort or another?" Ashley asked, perplexed.

Catherine nodded, "What I am saying is that the sister died not even a second after that thing left."

Ashley felt a shiver run up her spine. "That's sick. My God, where in the hell were you when this happened?"

Catherine smiled faintly as the memory came to the surface. "I was in Louisiana for a very short period of time after I was vowed. I was sent to teach way back in the bayou with a few dozen sisters and a handful of Jesuit priests. Sister Angelica was the only nursing sister on our mission.

"We were there for almost a month when a very sick child came to us. Sister Angelica was the first to see the child, but before she could get the doctor to see him, he died in her arms. The mother was furious. She screamed curses as she disappeared into the swamps.

"A few days later, Sister Angelica got sick,

mentally as well as physically. She saw demons everywhere. She spiked high temperatures, and then her body cooled off to well below the normal range. She went into convulsions that were so violent it took four men to hold her down.

"It was then that the priests decided to try an exorcism. Myself and one other sister were called in to assist with it. And I told you what happened after that.

"I don't know what it was. All I know is that stories began to surface out of the bayou a day or so after Angelica died. People said that she was cursed by a mambo, a voodoo witch that lived back in the swamps somewhere. All I know is what I saw, and what I saw was very much like what attacked us just now. Death in its most evil form was conjured, and we were the targets of it's rage."

Silence hung over the women as each was lost in her own thoughts.

Amanda found them like that when she came downstairs a few hours later. "What's going on?" Amanda asked.

Ashley raised her hand, "You wouldn't believe it if we told you."

Amanda shrugged and left the kitchen. She had her chores to do before breakfast. She wondered what the women had been doing all night. They looked as pale as sheets. She went about her chores.

Olivia was more tired than when she had gone to bed. And she felt cold even though the morning was already warm. She pulled on a sweater, which helped very little. Her stomach flip-flopped, and she felt nauseated.

She made her way down to the kitchen to prepare breakfast. Patricia followed her in and started helping. Olivia was grateful to her friend. If it had been up to her, she would have just stayed in bed. A hearty country breakfast was set on the table by the time the girls made their way down the stairs.

Jackie glanced at Emily and knew the suggestion she had so carefully planted in her mind had not stuck. The High Priestess would not be pleased to hear about this failure. She looked away when Emily glared at her. She began plotting another scheme. These women were even stronger than the prayers of the High Priestess. *Therefore,* Jackie thought, *they must die by physical means.*

Emily stared down the child and tried to probe her thoughts, but a barrier there prevented penetration. *That's okay,* Emily thought, *we'll deal with you when we get to you.*

She had told friends about what had happened in the forest and cautioned all of them to stay away from all the girls. Emily wasn't sure how many of them were involved with the happenings.

When Olivia and Patricia joined them at the breakfast table, there was a solemn mood of silence. Emily began to take a bite of her pancakes when something caught her eye. The milk in Olivia's glass had taken on a slightly green tinge. She closed her eyes and reopened them only to find that the color had not faded.

Olivia reached for the milk, hoping that it's coolness would soothe her stomach. "Don't drink that," Emily said suddenly from the other end of the table. Olivia looked startled as she placed the glass back on the table.

All eyes were on Emily, including Jackie's. "Why shouldn't she drink it?' Jackie asked.

Emily glared at the seemingly innocent child for a moment, and then she turned her eyes to Olivia whose face was bleached with fear. Emily reached for the glass and brought it toward her. She examined the milk carefully. "It's been poisoned. Someone has been systematically poisoning you for a long time."

Amanda laughed. "Well, that's about the craziest thing I ever heard. Come on, this is fresh milk from the cow. I get the milk from the cow and bring it in here. No one touches the milk but my mother and me."

Emily raised her hand. "Hold on, now. Where do you keep the milk bucket when you're not using it?"

Amanda contemplated not answering but thought better of it. Her mother was sick, and no one knew why. Even when Olivia had relented the one time and sought medical help, the doctor couldn't figure out what was ailing her. "I leave it out in the barn. It is covered at night so that no dirt or anything gets in it. What are you driving at?"

As clear as if she were there, Emily saw how the poison got into the milk.

During the middle of the night after the lights went out at the school, someone opened the lid of the bucket and sprinkled something inside.

Emily felt almost faint as the image slipped from her. "Arsenic. It's arsenic they're using," Emily said, finding her chair behind her.

Patricia turned to Olivia. "My God, that is virtually untraceable even after death unless someone was looking for it specifically."

"Are you sure? Are you absolutely sure?" Amanda asked, reaching for her mother's hand.

Emily nodded. "There's no time to waste. You have to get her out of here or she'll die. They already know that I know about the arsenic. Next time they may be a bit bolder in trying to kill your mother." Emily turned her attention to where Jackie had sat. As she had suspected, the girl was gone. She had slipped out unnoticed.

"Go now. Take her to the hospital and then have her transferred out of town to some place where they can't find her. Time is running out, and the doctors need to give her something to neutralize the poison." Emily turned her attention to her friends. "We need to go see Bethany O'Connor and hope that she can help us put a stop to it."

"Put a stop to what?" Ashley asked in confusion.

"To what might be the end of the time sequence as we know it. If they're successful, all of time might change forever." Emily rose from her chair with purpose now. She felt strong and afraid. She had seen many things in her life, but that which waited for them behind the hood of the High Priestess was something beyond anything she had ever encountered.

THIRTEEN

Jackie ran as fast as she could through the forest. She stumbled and fell a few times, scraping her knees and arms. Blood trickled from the wounds as her legs pumped. Her lungs felt like they would burst under pressure. She did not slow down until she was a little less than a mile from the school and knew no one was following her.

She sat on a log to catch her breath. Her mind twirled with thoughts. The most horrifying was the realization that the High Priestess was not so powerful as she let on.

Jackie sat naked and vulnerable before her own impotent God. The power that she had longed for, manipulated for, and killed for slipped through her hands like water. The harder that she tried to get it back, the more that power escaped her grasp.

Slowly, like the snake that slithered silently around her feet, a thought came to her. At first it was so tiny that she left it behind, but it grew and soon filled her whole mind. It was almost as if the Horned God that she served sat next to her on the log and spoke her thoughts. Jackie smiled as insanity clouded her eyes. She listened intently. *Yes,* she agreed. *It is time to take the crown of silver and become the next High Priestess of the coven.* Before she could ask how, her God whispered plans to her, great plans that would make her the next High Priestess.

Jackie thought she saw someone sitting very close to her, but she shoved the image out of her mind. She knew that it was the Horned God speaking to her, not the strange man who followed her around. He scared her with his shadowy form and strange dress. No, it was her God who spoke to her and no one else.

Jackie rose and wiped away the sweat that burned her eyes. A smile touched her lips. The words of the God were still fresh in her mind. She moved slowly at first and then picked up pace. It was already closing in on noon, and she had very little time to do as he God had said.

* * * * *

126

After Amanda and Olivia left for the hospital, the others climbed into Patricia's car to find Bethany.

The bear heard the women coming and stood up on two legs just outside the cabin door, which was open. None of the women opened their car doors until Bethany appeared in the door frame of the cabin and the bear sauntered off into the woods.

As Emily approached, she noticed that the old woman was blind. Emily took the woman's hand in her own. Bethany smiled, "It is good to finally meet you in the flesh, Emily."

"How did you know it was me?" Emily asked, though she already knew of the power that the old woman possessed.

Bethany smiled, "I heard your step. And right behind you is your friend Ashley." Again, the woman thrust out her hand.

Ashley took her hand in her own. She felt almost as though she were standing in the presence of greatness. The woman had risked her own well-being to save their lives last night. And her knowledge was great.

Bethany greeted all of them by name and took their hands in her own. More than just a greeting, she was feeling their auras and their thoughts. What she had to do later would require the strongest and the bravest. She would not risk using anyone who glimmered even slightly with wavering loyalty or dishonest intentions. She relaxed a bit after each woman came to her. Each one was strong with her own powers, but all of their powers separated would not be enough to stop what lay ahead. The women

127

must join their powers to stop the actions of the High Priestess.

When all of her guests were seated around the wooden table in the small kitchen, Bethany said, "Forget all that you know, or think you know, about witchcraft. Books and movies tend to twist and shape the ways of Wicca. I'll try to tell you the truth as I know it." Bethany smiled, and her face lit up. "I'll be giving you a crash course on the wondrous powers of true Wicca, and the blackest realities of the darker witchcraft that challenges us this hour."

Teri pulled into the driveway of the school. The building seemed to loom over the vast clearing in the forest. She was alone. A chill ran through her. She explored all of the possibilities of what could have happened since she had spoken with Ashley the night before.

She wanted to back out of the driveway, follow the dirt road back to the main road, and drive into Wallace for a cup of coffee. Fear twisted in her gut. Sometimes she wondered about her attraction to Emily. Spooky places and weird people attracted Emily like a moth to a flame, but Teri wanted absolutely nothing to do with any of it. The Windlow mansion had been enough to last her for a lifetime. Yet here she was again. But she reminded herself that she was here for a damned good reason. Ashley had not gone into much detail on the phone, but Teri had sensed that Emily was in some sort of trouble.

"And here I am," Teri announced to the air. She

did not see the curtain move away from a window on one of the upper floors of the school. She did not feel the eyes that scrutinized her from above. She pondered her next move.

"Yes, and there you are," a voice said against the window. She could almost hear Teri's thoughts as though the wind were her ears. She let the curtain slide back into place and moved quietly through the apartment that Amanda shared with her mother. The woman's arrival was quite unexpected but also convenient. It would fit into her plans nicely. A smile touched her lips as she softly shut the door and moved down the staircase to greet Teri as she came in.

Bethany brought the steaming mug of tea to her lips. She sighed before she sipped the contents. "As it hurt none, do what thou wilt. That is the one and only rule in Wicca. I have known for some time that this rule has been broken by someone very close to me, close to my heart. I taught her everything she knew, and then she moved beyond the realm of Wicca and entered into another. The blackest sort of magic. She didn't know that I knew about her until the vision that Emily and I shared the other evening. And now she'll try to kill us all."

Patricia absentmindedly picked up sugar granules with her fingertips. "Who is she?"

Bethany rose from the table, "It doesn't matter now who she is. She has been lost to me for a long time. What does matter is what will happen tonight if we don't join together and stop her."

"What was it that we saw? I understood some of it, but the hows and whys escape me," Emily said as she tried to concentrate on the vision.

Bethany returned to the table with a large tome in her hands. The cover was very old and made from heavy cardboard. The binding was intact, though yellowed and cracking with age. Bethany opened the pages and Patricia gasped.

"My God, is that a Book of Shadows?" Patricia asked, reaching out her fingers to touch the ancient pages. "I've never seen one before."

Bethany nodded. "It belonged to my mother and to her mother before that. Each of us has added her own wisdom and knowledge to the book. I had to copy this book into my own because I was born without my sight, but this is the original. I used to know every line on every page before my memory started leaving me."

Patricia took the book from Bethany. The women gathered around her to see the many pages of wisdom dating back hundreds of years.

"They're trying to bring the past to the present. They're trying to rip a hole in time. That was what they were doing when Amanda shot the High Priestess. They are going to try it again tonight. This night represents the Sabbat of Lughnasadh, August Eve, the earth harvest. Her magic will be potent and lethal."

Catherine looked up from the pages. "What are they after? Why would they want to tear a hole in time?"

"They are seeking two things. In pulling the past with the present, those who lived and died in the mine will become flesh again just as they were moments before they died. The High Priestess will then enter that other time and bring the women out of the mine, but not through the portal of time. The mine will cave in as it did before, but the women will be alive.

"Moments after that my father will ride up with his followers as he did in the past. He seeks revenge and he will have it. He has waited for a long time on the other side of death for this moment. He has chosen his instrument carefully and has trained her with all the powers of hell. They will be successful."

Ashley scratched her head. "Now wait a minute, you're telling me that it's possible to open a portal from one time to another and that people can walk through said portal and change history like that?"

Bethany nodded. "Believe me child, I have seen things in this lifetime that I would not have believed could be done. There are powers beyond your wildest imagination out there waiting for people to tap into them. The universe teems with life and the power to end it."

"What kind of revenge is he seeking? What could those women possibly have done to him? And who is he?" Ashley fired the questions so fast that Bethany had to raise her hand to still them.

"Jacob Wittacker the Third," Patricia announced before Bethany could say anything.

"That is correct," Bethany said. "He was my father though I never knew the man. He raped my mother before she left New York with Eliza in 1899. My mother was Alexandria O'Connor. She and Eliza Wittacker died in the mine that now sits on the Michaels's land.

"A woman named Rosalind Mary Lynn Tippton

came to my father in secret shortly after Christmas of 1898 and told him about a very strange affair between my mother, who everyone thought was a man at the time, and his wife Eliza. Between my father and Mrs. Tippton, my mother's secret remained intact until the spring of 1899 when he went to see her one night after a play. My mother was one of the finest actors of the stage at that time.

"He went into her dressing room and told her all that he knew, including the love affair that had started between his wife and my mother. The two argued about her identity until he grabbed my mother by her shirt and ripped it off her body. He raped her violently and beat her until she was barely breathing. Until the day that she died, she bore a mark that he put on her.

"Unbeknownst to Eliza, my father was a member of a cult of witches in New York who dabbled in the darker side of magic. Some today would call it Satanism. He was endowed with a great many powers and was feared in his coven.

"My mother received her gifts from her mother, who had received them from her mother. The Wicca, the healing magic. My mother was strong in her own right, but she didn't have the strength to stop Wittacker. He had planned on killing Eliza, using her as some sort of sacrifice to his god.

"My mother knew of his plans. Within a week, she brought her brother and Eliza to Idaho and bought some land near Placer Creek. We lived there until he found out through his magic where we were. On the night of the cave-in, he came seeking revenge. He had lost most of his powers as a High Priest when the dark side of the universe turned its face from him. He was in a rage; he still is. He wants the satisfaction of killing the one person that he could never manipulate with his powers. He wants to take my mother to the belly of hell with him. That is why the portal of time must be opened. It is the only way that he can confront her in the flesh and tear out her soul with his magic. He has waited all these years for the right person to come along. Through her he has grown strong again, and through her he will live again."

"At the very most, that would make you ninety-six years old," Ashley said figuring the math in her head. "How do you know so much if you were just a baby when your mother died?"

Bethany raised her brows, "Age means nothing, child, in the scheme of things. From the time that my mother died until this very day, she has been with me. I can see her in my dreams. She told me where to find her Book of Shadows, and she taught me all that I know today."

"What happened to your uncle? Did he die in the cave-in that took your mother and Eliza?" Emily asked, watching the old woman's face.

"My uncle and I escaped. He hid me in a hole underneath some floorboards in the barn. He watched as the men rode up and ransacked the house and barn.

"After the men left and he was certain it was safe to move from the protection of the hole, he went to see the old midwife who helped birth me. She took us into her home in secret. In fact, this is where she lived until she died many years ago.

"Shortly after my uncle brought me here, he left to find work. He worked for the railroad for a number of years until the great fire in 1910. Because of a drought that year, three million acres of land were burned. It was like looking into the mouth of hell. The old midwife and I stayed, though he came several times and begged us to leave. During that time I learned one of the greatest pieces of magic in my life — the Cone of Power. It was the only way we escaped being burned to death.

"My uncle died in that fire. He worked with the other men to extinguish the flames until they were surrounded by the fires up on the west fork of Placer Creek. He left behind his wife, whom I never knew, and two daughters.

"His daughter Rosie died at a young age a few years after he died, and his other daughter, Emma, married a man and moved to Jackson Springs. She died not too long ago at the age of eighty-eight. Her daughter came back here to live, and her son went back to New York. Ginny traced our family tree and found out about me. I got to know her quite well before she died.

"She would come up here in the summer and bring her two granddaughters. They didn't know what to call me, so I just said call me grandmother. Danielle still comes to see me almost every day."

Emily noticed a look of pain twist the old face for a few seconds before it was swallowed up in the lines and wrinkles. She knew what Bethany was thinking, and Emily remembered the vision. She knew the face that Bethany was seeing and why it had caused her such pain. She reached out and touched the woman's hand. She could not imagine what it was going to be like to have to face someone so loved in a battle that would surely end in death.

"Emma's son was Amanda's grandfather. That is why I sent the note to Sam those many years ago. I had to warn him, but now it's too late for that. Sam is gone, and now Olivia is in danger," Bethany said. She looked like a woman defeated.

As Catherine opened her mouth to ask a question, the door to the cabin opened. Everyone except for Bethany turned toward the doorway. Within the frame stood Jackie.

Emily was the first to move toward the girl until she saw a shotgun in her hands. Emily froze in her tracks as Jackie came inside the cabin and looked from one woman to the other. A sinister grin played across her face.

Ashley rose from her chair and she slid protectively in front of Catherine. She had not imagined that it would be Jackie whom the cult sent to kill them, and she had not thought that it would happen this way.

Bethany rose from her chair and turned toward the girl who moved quietly toward the women. In her mind, Bethany called for Keva. "What is the meaning of this, child?"

Jackie smiled. Insanity glazed her eyes. She flashed from one woman to the other, all the while holding the gun steady in her hands. It was time.

Teri could stand the suspense no longer and opened the car door. She moved across the gravel driveway and up to the door. She thought about knocking but figured since it was a school knocking would be inappropriate.

She opened one side of the heavy wooden doors and was greeted by a terrible quietness. "Hello," she called into the hallway. Her voice echoed around the school. Tentatively, she stepped in and allowed the door to shut behind her.

A woman stepped from the shadows beyond and startled Teri. "Hello," the woman greeted her, moving to close the distance between the two. Her hand reached out in front of her.

Teri smiled and took the woman's hand in her own. The woman's touch was cool and brief. "Hello," Teri said again. "I'm Teri, Emily's friend. I heard that she was ill, and I came to get her."

The smile that touched the woman's face worried Teri slightly. There was no mirth in the smile. It was merely cool and uninviting. "I think, my dear, that you are a lot more than friends with Emily, but that doesn't matter. My name is Danielle. I'm, uh, friends with Amanda and her mother, Olivia. I was just looking for them when I saw you pull in."

"Oh," Teri said, following the woman to the large dining room. She felt jumpy around the woman. From the way that Emily had talked, Danielle was friendly and warm, but this woman was cool and aloof.

"Sit here, I'll get you a cup of tea, and we can talk about your friend Emily and the others. They should be back soon." Before Teri could answer, the woman had disappeared behind the doors of the kitchen.

She returned a few minutes later with two tall glasses of iced tea in her hands. She set one in front of Teri.

"I believe that Emily is doing much better than

yesterday, though I haven't seen her since then. She was quite ill, in fact, but she seems to have recovered nicely." The woman drew a long sip from her glass.

The iced tea looked cool and inviting. Teri sipped from the glass. She tasted a slight bitterness that she didn't recognize. She dismissed it as being some sort of different tea. She didn't think about it again until her thoughts became fuzzy. She found it hard to follow the conversation.

"You know, I am rather glad you came, Teri. You are going to be quite valuable to me tonight. Don't worry, you'll just sleep for a while. I didn't poison you or anything so barbaric as that." The woman talked on, but Teri lost track of what she was saying. She tried to rise from her chair. The last thought that she had before the blackness closed in was, *What in the hell am I doing here?* From somewhere far off she heard a woman laughing. The laughter became like ice wedged in her brain, and her blood ran as cold.

FOURTEEN

Olivia slipped in and out of consciousness at the hospital. With robust fervor, the doctors and nurses buzzed around her, working as quickly as their knowledge allowed. A few times, one of the nurses would leave the room and speak with Amanda. She was getting worse, one nurse had reported.

Amanda sat with her head in her hands and waited for the worst. She had told the doctor what she had suspected, and he looked at her like she had gone insane. Only after she had insisted and the police had tests run on the milk sample did the medical staff move in that direction. Meanwhile, precious time had slipped away, and her mother was dying.

Olivia felt herself looming above the room, and when she opened her eyes she saw her body below her. The nurses and doctor were working at a frantic pace that she could not understand. Nothing made sense to her as she watched. What was their hurry? And why was it so important that this body live? She felt free and light. She wanted to stay that way.

From the corner of her eye, Olivia saw movement in the room that didn't seem like it belonged there. She willed herself to float toward it. She recognized the face of the young man who stood waiting for her.

"Sam," she heard her voice say, though she had only thought it.

The young man smiled at her as she went into his embrace. It had been so long since she had felt this way. "My love," he said as he embraced her.

"What's happening?" Olivia asked as she looked back toward the table where her body lay. She could see the heart monitor and someone putting the paddles to her body's chest. The shock caused the green line to bow and jump for a bit only to have it straighten out again.

"It's time for you to come with me into the next world, my love," Sam said, holding her hand. The thought caused a touch of fear. She knew what was happening to her.

"Mandy will be fine. All things will work out for her, I can assure you of that. Come with me now. It's time." Sam put his arm around her as a shaft of light appeared from the ceiling and invited them. Olivia thought she heard the splendid voice of God calling her by name from the beam of light. She wanted to go.

After one more look around the room, she knew that it was time for her to move on into the light. She felt exhilarated as she moved toward the soft glow. A feeling of ecstasy filled her with anticipation as she became a part of the light and disappeared into it.

Jackie leveled the shotgun against her shoulder and aimed it at Bethany. She was trying to focus her mind on pulling the trigger when Keva came suddenly from behind her and pushed her over with all of her weight.

The shotgun went off, and tiny BBs splattered the wall near Bethany's head. The women were frozen in their spots as they watched the great brown bear crush the girl with her weight. Keva did not move until Bethany approached them.

Jackie gasped for air as Bethany pulled her to her feet. "It's time for answers," she said simply as she led Jackie to one of the chairs. Keva remained close to her master.

It became very clear that the girl had lost her mind as she babbled on and on about nothing. Bethany probed her thoughts as she rambled on.

"He's lying to you, Jackie. He has no power, and he will not make you the High Priestess when this is all done. There is nothing but destruction and death for you if you follow him. Eternal pain and hell. That will be his reward for you. Can you hear me, child?" Bethany touched the girl's face. Her hands were warm and soothing. From somewhere far away, Jackie responded.

"Please help me," the girl blubbered as tears washed the dirt from her face.

Bethany talked smoothly and evenly. "I need to know about the last time that the High Priestess tried to open a hole in time."

Jackie's eyes glazed over again. "Something went wrong. Something went very wrong. She had it planned out so well, and then Amanda came outside and shot her."

"Shot whom," Ashley questioned.

Jackie did not turn to the sound of the voice when she answered. Her gaze stared out into the void. "The High Priestess."

Ashley straightened her back and moved away from the group that hovered near the girl. "That's impossible," she declared.

"She has powers. She is protected by the Horned God for as long as she serves him," Jackie said in a monotone voice. There was no hint of emotion.

Bethany crossed her brows. "There is no God, only him that calls her to do these things. I know you know that. He was a man at one time until he died and passed to the other side."

"No, that's not true," Jackie said. "I've heard the voice of the Horned God. He's real."

Bethany raised her hands in defeat. She moved her questions back to the night that the High Priestess was shot. "Who was the sacrifice that night?"

"Christine," Jackie answered simply.

Catherine felt a chill. "How could that have been? She committed suicide."

Jackie shook her head. "It was to appear that way, but she was the one who offered herself to the High Priestess that night. After it was all over, I helped bring her body into the house. We hung her from the rafters. It was planned that way. Christine even wrote her own suicide note." Jackie giggled.

"My God," Patricia said, bringing her hand to her mouth.

Catherine pulled away from the group and joined Ashley, who was moving toward the door of the cabin. She fought a wave of nausea and longed to breathe fresh air again.

Jackie's eyes darted to the door. In a flash of movement, she bolted for the exit. In that same moment, Keva sprang from her place and chased after her.

"No," Bethany called from where she stood. "Let her go."

"What do you mean you're sorry," Amanda demanded angrily. Tears loomed in the darkness of her eyes. Her fists were knotted up at her sides.

"It was just too late for your mother. Her heart gave out. I am surprised that she lived as long as she did with the poison milling around in her system. Listen, we tried everything we could." The doctor shoved her hands into her pockets. She hated this worst of all. A look of concern stitched across her kindly face. She took Amanda by the elbow. "Come with me."

Amanda followed Dr. Jerilynn Rutherford down the hall. Shortly after Amanda and Olivia had arrived, she had stepped out of the emergency room to give Amanda an initial assessment on her mother and as quickly disappeared behind the doors again. Now, this doctor was telling her that Olivia was dead.

Doctor Rutherford opened the door to a small, heavily shadowed room, and Amanda followed her inside. The woman shut the door and sat in one of the chairs before she spoke again. "Look, arsenic, if that's what it was, is virtually untraceable except through an autopsy, in some cases. Your mother fought the best that she could. There was simply not enough time to reverse the damage of the poison or to determine what the poison was. Realistically, your mother was living on borrowed time. Right now, I would have to say that she died of heart failure, and nothing else." The doctor touched Amanda's hand briefly. "I'm sorry. I really am," she said with compassion.

"That's just not good enough, damn it. That's just not good enough," Amanda yelled. Emotions exploded within her so quickly that she couldn't grasp any long enough to feel it. Her anger showed. It was the one emotion she knew would carry her through this.

Doctor Rutherford rambled on about the police being notified and an autopsy needing to be performed, but Amanda barely heard her. A few tears spilled as Doctor Rutherford left the room to allow Amanda a few minutes before the police began their questioning.

Five hours after Olivia died in the emergency room, Doctor Rutherford found that the contents in the milk bucket did contain small doses of arsenic.

Time slid by as the police asked questions and papers were placed in front of Amanda for her signature. She felt numb and wanted to leave. She wanted to go back home where things were familiar and comforting. She wanted her mother to be there waiting and for this nightmare to be over. The doctor had to be wrong.

The woman dragged Teri to the truck she had hidden in the barn. She carelessly lifted Teri up and tossed her like a sack of potatoes in the bed of the truck. The woman figured that Teri would probably wake with a headache anyway, so a few knocks and bruises would be the least of her worries.

The woman started the truck and sped out of the barn, onto the driveway, and away from the looming shadows of the school. She checked off the necessary preparations. Nothing could stop her now. After tonight, she would be the richest woman and the most powerful in all the county. The price she had to pay did not matter in the end. All that mattered was the gold that waited to be mined in that shaft on what would become her land. After all, she was of the O'Connor line, and the land rightfully belonged to her. The woman laughed loudly as she drove haphazardly over the terrain.

In the back of the truck, Teri bounced around like a rag doll. She dreamed she was in a black sea that reached for miles upward. She tried once to swim to the surface, and as her head broke the surface of consciousness she called Emily's name before she slid back into blackness.

Emily stood up straight. Her face took on an expression of fear. She could hear Teri from far away as a flash crossed her mind.

The school loomed in the background. Movement. Her body ached, and blood ran down her face from a cut on her forehead. And then blackness.

"The bitch has got Teri," Emily announced from her dreamlike state.

"What?" Ashley asked, moving across the tiny room toward her friend.

"She's got Teri. I saw it. We've got to find her. She's in danger. I could smell death all around her." Emily's voice rose in panic as she reached for her purse and headed for the door.

Bethany stood. She had seen the image too. "No, child, you won't be able to find her, not yet anyway. She's not in any immediate danger. We need to plan carefully, now. Too many lives are in her hands."

Emily felt the old woman's hand on her shoulder. She could feel her muscles relax under the touch. "But, Teri —" Emily's eyes pleaded.

A smile touched Bethany's lips. "Your love will be enough to protect her for now, I promise you that much. Listen to me. Right now what Teri needs is for you to keep your head and to prepare for what will be. Otherwise, there will be no chance for any of us."

It was close to evening when Amanda opened the door to the apartment she had shared with her mother. She fought the urge to run as she shut the door behind her. In an instant, her eyes picked out the little things that belonged to her mother.

Her sweater was tossed casually over the arm of the sofa, as though she had planned on putting it on later when the night cooled. Olivia had left her book on the coffee table with a bookmark in place.

"She'll never know how the book ended," Amanda said to herself as she touched the green, fabric cover. She wanted a drink so bad that her soul ached. She had never known such pain.

Amanda moved through the quiet apartment looking at her mother's things. She touched everything that her mother had touched, as if touching her things would be enough to wake her from the nightmare she was having.

After she had made her way through the entire apartment with the slowness of one whose sharp-edged memories cut deep, Amanda sank wearily into the overstuffed couch. Tears sprang into her eyes. "Oh, God, no," Amanda cried out into the empty void that surrounded her. "Mother," she screamed. The pain inside her heart threatened to consume her sanity.

* * * * *

Stephanie sat in her room and hugged herself as she rocked on the bed. She had heard that Olivia had gone to the hospital and when Amanda came home alone with the look of absolute loss on her face, Stephanie knew that Olivia was dead.

She felt a pain that she could not drink or drug away. Her mind scolded her. She had, in her own way, loved Olivia like a grandmother. And now the old woman was dead, and it was her fault.

If she had told someone about the strange things that were going on, Olivia would still be alive. She recalled the times that she had followed Jackie out of the school and had seen her tampering with the milk bucket in the barn. At the time she had thought nothing of it. Since Jackie was infamous for playing jokes on occasion, especially when Christine was still alive, she had thought it was a prank.

Christine. She was the reason Stephanie hadn't said anything to anyone. Christine had not committed suicide like everyone said. She was murdered.

Stephanie jumped as the door to her room slammed open. At first she did not recognize Jackie as she came through the door. The girl was covered with dirt and small patches where blood had dried on her knees and elbows. A gash lined her forehead.

"What the hell?" Stephanie breathed in alarm. She rose from her bed. She was not afraid until she saw Jackie's eyes.

Jackie heard the voice of her God speaking over her shoulder. In fact, she heard the voices of millions whispering to her, but her God's voice was the clearest.

"Jackie, what's going on?" Stephanie questioned as her eyes scanned the room for an escape route.

Jackie obeyed the voice and shut the door quietly behind her. A smile touched her lips. Her eyes sparkled like the edge of the sharpened knife she held in her hand. She moved with the ease of someone who knew what must be done and felt comfortable with her decision to do it. The fear in Stephanie's eyes made her pause.

"Jackie, what in the fuck do you think you're doing?" Stephanie said, raising her voice in the hope that her words would travel to the apartment one floor up.

"Kill her," the raspy voice over Jackie's shoulder demanded. "Kill her. She knows what you have done. She'll tell everyone what you did to Christine. Kill her, now!"

Jackie raised the knife and rushed Stephanie without warning. Stephanie moved quickly. The blow grazed her arm. Her eyes darted desperately to the door. She would have to get through Jackie.

Jackie moved purposely toward her victim while the voice screeched and hollered in her ears. "Kill her, kill her," voices chanted in tongues so ancient they had been long forgotten.

Stephanie watched Jackie advance. She had one chance to escape, and to do so she had to allow Jackie to come dangerously close. Her muscles trembled as she coiled them in preparation.

Jackie swung the knife wildly. Stephanie raised her leg in the air and hit Jackie in the chest at full force. The knife flew out of Jackie's hand and skidded across the floor as she recoiled from the blow and landed squarely on her back. She lay gasping for air while Stephanie moved quickly past her and out the door.

Jackie felt herself being raised to her feet by cold, invisible hands. "Get up, you bitch, or I will destroy you as you stand," the voice of the Horned God said roughly.

Jackie stood, bewildered by the blow she had received. She covered her ears to shut out the voices that droned on beside her. "No," she cried, running from the room and down the stairs. She ran out the door of the school and into the silence of the forest beyond. On her heels she could hear the laughter of a legion of demons that followed in pursuit.

Stephanie ran in a daze. She wasn't sure where her feet were leading her until she stopped short at the door to Amanda's apartment. All she could think about was that Amanda had a gun, and a person with a gun could defend her better than she could defend herself outside in the forest where no one could hear her calling.

She opened the door so suddenly and with such force that it almost ripped the hinges from the frame. With a small voice that barely squeaked out of her mouth, Stephanie called for Amanda.

"What the hell?" Amanda demanded as she rose from the couch. Her face was wet with tears that she dried quickly on her sleeve. "What the hell is going on here?" she asked as she approached the frightened girl who stood in the doorway. It wasn't until she was closer that she saw the blood trickling from the girl's arm.

"Stephanie, what happened?" Amanda asked as she pulled the girl into the kitchen where she pressed a kitchen towel to the wound.

"Jackie did it. She has flipped out. She killed your mother and Christine and God only knows who else. Now she wants to kill me because I know too much," Stephanie said in one breath.

Amanda raised her hand. "Hold on. Slow down, for God's sake. Now what the hell does my mother have to do with Jackie? And what is this about her killing Christine?"

Stephanie gave a nervous and frightened look at the door. A tiny bit of relief touched her when she saw that Jackie was not there.

Amanda followed her gaze, and a nervous look shot across her face. "Come with me," Amanda said, pulling the girl with her. The pair moved to the second bedroom of the apartment.

Amanda cursed under her breath when she discovered that the 20-gauge shotgun was nowhere to be found in her room. Quickly, she searched her nightstand for the .357 magnum that she had hidden there. She checked to assure there was still a round in the cylinder before she snapped it shut.

Stephanie's arm had stopped bleeding, and Amanda bandaged the gash as the girl told her everything she knew. Amanda's face grew tight with anger as each detail was laid out in front of her.

"Why in the hell didn't you tell me sooner? My mother might still be alive right now if I had known," Amanda blamed as she rolled the gauze up and put it back into its box.

Stephanie stepped back from Amanda. "I thought she was playing a prank like she used to do when she first came here. I had no idea it was serious. And with Christine, I woke up the night they said she committed suicide. I heard something fall in

Christine's room, so I got up and went down the hall. Her room was very dark, and I couldn't see anything at first.

"After a second or two, I saw Jackie and someone else placing a rope around Christine's neck. She was still alive because I saw her moving her hand slightly to resist them. After that I have no recall. For a long time I didn't even remember what I just told you. I am sorry about your mom. I loved her, too. She was the only person who ever treated me like I wasn't just a child." Stephanie reached out her hand and touched Amanda on the shoulder.

Amanda shook as she sobbed. Through her tears she said, "It's okay. It's not your fault, I know that." She allowed Stephanie into her arms, and the two cried in unison as the long shadows of evening began to give way to the blackness of the night.

FIFTEEN

Teri woke with a headache that ran from her eyes to the base of her neck. The pain made every muscle in her body scream. In the blackness that surrounded her, Teri tried to make sense of what had happened. Her mind felt soggy, and she found that to probe too long made her head hurt worse.

She lay still and allowed her thoughts to come slowly. When she realized that she was not at home but somewhere in Idaho, a panic began to rise in her. Someone had attacked her inside the school. She struggled between consciousness and wakefulness. She knew she must remain awake or she might never wake again.

A warm wind touched her face. *I'm outside.* Some jagged edges were cutting into her back. She felt the area beside her. Whatever she was lying on was warm to the touch. Her hands and legs were bound; frantically, she pulled against the bonds, but found them secure.

She moved her head from side to side. In the pale wash of the moonlight, she saw the mouth in the side of a mountain. *The mine shaft,* she thought, as her memories returned. The one that Ashley spoke of on the phone. *Emily,* her mind screamed, and she attempted to sit up, but the cords bound her to the spot.

Teri fought to free herself until she saw the black figure approaching. It stood out even in the blackness of the night.

"Don't struggle," the voice said. Teri winced with fear. "It will soon be over, and you will be free," the voice of a woman said from within the folds of the robe.

Teri felt a chill run through her. She thought of screaming in the hope that someone would hear her, but the voice spoke again, silencing the scream.

"It will do you no good to cry out. No one is here to listen. And your Emily, she'll soon join you on the other side." The figure laughed as other figures dressed in black came from the shadows near the barn, from the schoolhouse, and from the sides of the mine.

The figures chanted softly in words Teri could not understand. A warm wind came from the south as the robed woman raised her hand. A flash of lightning lit the sky from a distance. As Teri watched the figures moving into a semicircle around her and the mouth of the mine, Teri carefully moved her hands in the bindings. She had one chance, but first she had to break the cords around her hands.

Amanda left Stephanie at the hospital and drove home again. The .357 magnum rode in the passenger seat next to her. She chewed nervously on her fingernails as she maneuvered her truck around the country road. She half expected Jackie to step out of the darkness with her shotgun and blow the front window to bits.

The grief for the loss of her mother was shoved back in her mind. According to Stephanie, the worst was not over yet. In fact, it had only just begun.

Amanda swerved suddenly as a horseman entered the road from out of the blackness on the left. He was followed by other horsemen. The wheels of her truck bit into the gravel road and snaked around for a few feet until she came to an abrupt stop.

She should have hit the man on the horse, but when she looked out the windshield she saw the man followed by his comrades ride into the blackness on the other side.

Amanda absorbed the scene that played out before her. The men were dressed in long black robes that rippled across the backs of their horses. The clothes that the men wore were not familiar to her; they looked like they were from an age long gone by.

Amanda shuddered as the last horseman disappeared. Her mind at first refused to believe what her eyes had witnessed. She had not hit the man on the horse, nor had he hit her. Rather, the man and horse rode right through the front end of her truck.

Bethany raised her head toward the night sky. The presence of evil permeated the night winds. It was time.

With a motion of her hand, the women gathered in a circle and joined hands. Bethany spoke, "Whatever happens, whatever you see or hear, do not break the circle or all will be lost." The women all nodded, but none spoke in agreement.

Ashley could feel Emily's hand tremble in her own. She knew what was on her mind. It was the same thing that had touched her mind several times as they walked a couple of miles through the brush and forest to this place. She could only hope that Teri was safe somewhere far from here.

Ashley could not help but wonder why Bethany had led them here. They stood on a clearing in the forest about an eighth of a mile away from the school. The old woman had said that this spot was consecrated and that evil could not touch the ground here.

Ashley wondered at the logic of that. She thought it would be best to call the police and let them handle it. At this suggestion, Bethany rose from her chair. "By the time the police came out, *if* they came out, it would be too late. Don't you understand yet what you are dealing with here? This is the worst kind of magic. It is spawned in the bottomless pit that some call hell. If she is not stopped on her own grounds tonight, she will never be stopped. Help me, Ashley, I need you to believe."

Ashley squeezed her eyes shut and tried to drive out her doubts. She knew she must believe in order for the Cone of Power to work. She could feel her muscles relaxing as she concentrated on nothingness. But deep within, one thought would not be shut out. Teri's voice called to her in fear.

Amanda moved her hand to the .357 magnum on the passenger seat. She put it on her lap before she started the truck. She scanned both doors to assure that they were locked. With her fear squelched, she put the truck into drive.

As the miles clicked by and the place of the incident moved farther and farther behind her, she began to relax again. She told herself there must be some logical explanation, though she really didn't believe it.

She allowed her mind to wander away from the horseman to something more pleasant. Danielle. She moved her hand to her jeans pocket and pulled out the note Danielle had written sometime earlier in the day. She had to cancel their date, but had asked if they could meet later on in the evening.

Amanda smiled. Even a piece of paper written on by Danielle seemed to send tingles around her body. She had to admit that she was in love with the woman. "Danielle," Amanda spoke aloud.

* * * * *

The High Priestess raised her head suddenly. Had someone called her true name from out of the darkness? She listened for a moment, but heard nothing but the wind as it blew harder through the trees. He was coming.

She opened her Book of Shadows and fought against the wind to keep the pages from moving. She found the entry she was looking for and placed a stone there to hold the pages.

When she raised her hand, the semicircle of people that surrounded her knelt in unison. "The time has come," she said, raising her voice to keep the wind from stealing her words. "Prepare yourselves."

From the folds of their robes, the followers pulled silver inverted pentacles with long, black, leather thongs and placed them around their necks. The silver glinted wildly in the flicker of the torch light.

Teri had managed to free one of her legs by rubbing the cord against the rock. She worked painstakingly on the other leg while the eyes were averted from her.

Fear was building a lump in her throat. She tried to quell the fear by thoughts of her daughter and Emily. She had to get free and hope that someone would come to help her. She could not envision herself dying on a rock somewhere in the forests of Idaho. "It just isn't in the cards," she recalled Emily saying.

"This is the celebration of Lughnasadh, August Eve, the earth harvest, and from the earth we will call forth the fruit of her belly that lies here." The High Priestess bowed her head then slowly rose to face the sky. She leveled her eyes and saw the riders coming. The sounds of the hooves sounded above the force of the wind.

To her left the school faded into the night and a cabin rose in its place, though it was a translucent image. The woman smiled and raised her hands. "Oh, God, I am your servant. Hear me now, I beg you. I have brought a sacrifice of blood to your table. If this pleases you, give me a sign of your appreciation," the woman called out.

Teri squirmed out on the rock unnoticed by anyone. She had freed her other leg as well as one of her hands. She had only to undo the other hand and she would be free. She paused when a flash of lightning illuminated the sky and touched down a few inches from the rock where she was bound. Panic welled inside her.

The circle of women began moving to the right. At first their feet were clumsy and the circle moved only a few inches from where it had begun. After a bit more trial and error, the women found themselves moving in unison with one another.

Bethany started to chant as the circle reached a momentum. "Goddess, Mistress of the Universe, Creator, and Life, we appeal to your goodness, this August Eve, and ask you to hear our cry in this wilderness, in this time of evil. Come to us and grant us your power from the living universe."

"Come and grant us your power from the living universe," Ashley repeated with the other women.

Her head suddenly began to spin, and she felt dizzy. The forest, illuminated by the moonlight, spun so fast around her that it became a blur. She shut her eyes and tried to regain momentum. If the other women had not held on to her, she would have gone crashing to the ground.

Over and over again the women repeated the same lines until the words lost their meaning entirely. Catherine could feel herself spinning like a top and suddenly taking flight into the night sky. Her eyes were closed, and she held on to the image. Bethany had said that the power of the chant was to set their souls dancing and that their bodies would follow.

Patricia felt her body growing taller and taller until she was among the stars. She imagined herself reaching out and touching one of the glittering orbs. She pulled it into her hand like a treasure that until now only God had touched. The star lost some of its glow for a moment and then sprang to life with brilliant colors that pierced the night. Patricia stood in wonder as the light ran down her arm and followed her body like a line to the earth far below.

Emily found herself wandering beyond the circle of women to the school. It was as though a power greater than her own resistance pulled her. She allowed it. Moving through a thick glob of jelly, she could see everything around her clearly. The schoolhouse no longer existed. In its place stood a cabin. From the chimney, a small stream of smoke curled its way to the sky. A woman dressed in a long black robe stood in front of the mine shaft. On a rock a stone weighed down the pages of an open book. In front of the woman was another rock, and on the rock was a person, though Emily could not make out who it was.

A group of men dressed in black robes with hoods down around the shoulders moved as if they were unaware of the happenings. One of the men watched the woman as she raised the small knife to the four corners of the earth. Emily knew who he was and why he was there. The past had come to the future and soon would be flesh again.

Emily moved as quickly as she could through the jelly. She had to see who was on the rock. As she drew closer, Emily could hear the woman say, "Accept this sacrifice from my hands to yours."

The sharp athame came down quickly and accurately, but the hand of the figure on the rock warded off the blow, which grazed the stone inches away from the figure's chest.

While the two struggled, Emily drew closer and a sharp cry pierced the night. "Teri," Emily cried. "Oh, my God, Teri." She tried to reach out and grab the robed woman's hand, but she could not hold on.

Teri struggled with the woman for a moment before the athame plunged into her chest. She felt as though the wind had been knocked out of her. There was no pain, but a burning sensation spread throughout her body. She grappled with consciousness, trying to stay awake. *If I can only stay awake, I won't die,* she thought. Somewhere in the darkness, she heard Emily crying, "No, No!"

The High Priestess dipped the bloody athame into a cup filled with herbs until the knife's edge was clean. She raised the cup above her head, and the coven began to chant. With the cup still raised above her head, the woman pointed to the four corners of the earth again. A clap of thunder filled the air with jagged sounds.

The man who had waited for so long in the deep void of time between death and life watched with enthusiasm. His hard eyes glinted with pleasure. Soon, he would be flesh again. Soon, he would lead this coven beyond anything they could imagine. He had seen places and things in the universe that his mind could not have fathomed while he was living.

He did not see the cone of bright, shifting colors grow from its pinpoint origin behind him in the nighttime sky. He did not see it as it funneled down and grew larger and larger until it touched the earth. And even if he had seen it, it would have meant nothing to him. This was one of the things that was kept from his knowing as he traveled in the void of time.

Bethany could feel the Cone of Power as it swirled around her. In the darkness of her world, her imagination went wild. She saw colors that only exist in the deepest part of God's imagination. Power surged within her. A voice called her name, and she responded. A warm wind lifted her hair off her shoulders and pulled her feet from the ground where she stood. Rain caressed her face and touched her blinded eyes.

"It is time, my child," the feminine voice said gently to her, and she knew the meaning behind the words. She had waited a long time to hear the voice that had called to her in her dreams as a child.

A smile touched her lips; her face shone with a brilliant light. "Yes, Mother Creator. It is time," Bethany said softly in response.

Without warning, Patricia plummeted to the ground at the fiery fury of a comet. Catherine's wings suddenly burned away, and she spiraled to the earth. Ashley was awakened harshly from a splendid dream that she would never remember or have again. Emily stumbled backwards and wrenched her hand out of Bethany O'Connor's grip.

Emily blinked a few times trying to clear a fog from her eyes. A look of pain and fury crossed her face. She remembered. With legs born of desperation, Emily rose and ran toward the mine. Bethany did not call after her or try to stop her, for she knew in an instant what the voice of the Mother had meant. She followed Emily with eyes that had been granted sight for the first and last time in this life.

Ashley watched Emily run toward the woods. She felt disoriented. From her mother to Catherine, she looked with eyes that refused to focus. She felt limp and useless as though all of her energy had been sucked out of her.

Catherine stared out into the woods where Emily, followed by Bethany, had run. Something had happened. She had seen Emily's face as she turned to run. *Teri,* Catherine thought with urgency, *something had happened to Teri.*

"Ashley, come on, we have to stop them," Catherine screamed as a clap of thunder boomed above. Ashley and Patricia followed Catherine with legs that felt like rubber.

* * * * *

Jackie stood in the silent, black shadows beside the schoolhouse. She held the 20-gauge shotgun in her hands. Her black robes kept her from being seen by the High Priestess or her demon companion who stood looking on greedily as she performed her blackest task yet.

Jackie's mind was cleared of that which had shadowed it. She no longer heard the God or his henchmen. She knew the truth. There never was a God, only him. She knew that he would have to die with her tonight. She moved as though her feet were weighted down with lead. "We have all come here to die tonight," she said as she raised the shotgun to her shoulder.

The High Priestess concentrated on her chant as she raised the cup one last time over her head. "Hear me, God. I am your most trusted servant. Relinquish to me your powers. Grant me the power to undo this cycle of time and enter into another so that era and this will become one in the same. To you I offer this sacrifice of blood."

When the woman lowered the cup, it was empty. She smiled. "It is granted," she said under her breath. From behind her, the air began to shift and mold itself. The face of the mine began to take on the shape and color of another age. A seam tore in half and revealed that which lay underneath.

The mouth of the mine was lit with the soft orange colors of dawn. From inside, women's voices could be heard, voices that had not uttered a word for nine decades.

The High Priestess smiled as she grabbed the flashlight she had brought with her. She and her followers crowded the mouth of the mine. Inside the mine were two figures. "Alexandria O'Connor," the woman called with a touch of joy in her voice.

A woman dressed in men's clothes moved toward her warily. "Who are you?" Alexandria demanded.

The High Priestess was about to reply when she heard a gunshot go off somewhere outside. She turned with alarm at the same moment the tear in time healed itself.

One of her followers lay in a pool of blood on the lawn. The woman looked up with disbelief. This was not supposed to happen. Not tonight, not after everything she had given away for this moment. Her eyes darted around for the assailant.

Jackie stood a few yards away. The girl leveled a shotgun at her head. A fury swelled inside the High Priestess as she straightened herself stiffly. "Kill the bitch," she growled.

The spirit of Jacob Wittacker stepped ahead of the coven. The wrath that burned in his eyes scared Jackie enough that she dropped the gun. She could not keep her eyes from his. She felt him probing into her thoughts. After a moment of resisting him, she let go. She had done what she had come to do. He would never be flesh again. And soon he, too, would stand naked before the God that created him and speak his sins in shame.

Her thoughts infuriated him and he let go of her mind. Jackie felt an excruciating pain that began in the back of her head and ran forward. Her brain felt like it was on fire. She fell to her knees and grabbed her head to extinguish the fire. From where she knelt, she saw the man turn away from her. "God, forgive me," she muttered as she collapsed on the ground. A moment later, she drew her final breath and departed.

Emily flung herself on Teri and ripped the cord that still bound her hand. She pulled the limp body to her breast and screamed and begged in desperation.

In a second, Bethany was beside her. The High Priestess looked on with amusement until she saw Bethany.

The High Priestess grabbed the athame in her hand and moved with purpose to the old woman. "I should have taken care of you a long time ago, Old Woman," she snarled.

"Is this all that is left of your magic that you have to turn a knife on me to take my life?" Bethany asked with calmness.

The High Priestess leapt toward Bethany with a fury borne of frustration and fear. The two women tore at each other as the High Priestess tried to drive the knife into Bethany's chest.

Bethany was weakening under the physical strength of the younger woman. She hoped desperately for a miracle. She knew she would not be able to take the punishing blows much longer. The knife had already found its mark once in her flesh. Another blow, Bethany feared, and her life would end without triumph.

A sound of a gun firing stopped the High Priestess from stabbing Bethany as she sat on top of the exhausted old woman. The headlights of a truck illuminated the whole terrible scene, and Amanda stepped out. She aimed the gun from one person to the next as she approached slowly.

The hood of the High Priestess had fallen back in the struggle, and the headlights revealed her identity.

"Danielle," Amanda breathed in horror and pain. "Oh, my God, no." Her feet refused to move.

A sneer crossed her face as she raised the knife high above her head.

"Don't," Amanda said weakly.

Emily stood up. Blood stained her shirt. "Kill her. Kill the murdering bitch," Emily said through clenched teeth.

"No, I can't," Amanda said through her tears. The .357 dropped to the ground. "I can't."

Laughter pealed through the air as the woman raised her knife again. "Good-bye," she said.

A shotgun blast shattered the air from the blackness beyond the headlights of Amanda's truck. The eyes of the High Priestess opened wide with shock. She looked down at her chest as the black robe she wore turned red with her own blood. *It wasn't supposed to end this way,* she thought desperately. She rose and stumbled to the rock where her Book of Shadows lay.

Another blast filled the night with a flash of finality. The woman was taken off her feet and thrown backward. Her eyes pleaded with the stars, last witnesses of her dying words. "It wasn't supposed to end this way," she murmured with her last breath.

Amanda turned from the grizzly scene that lay before her. A woman stepped into the light. She thought that she had lost her mind. "Danielle," she called as she felt herself grow faint.

Danielle reached out for her. "Yes," she said as she pulled Amanda to her. "It's over now. It's all over now."

The ambulance arrived within five minutes of Danielle's call from her police radio. Teri and Bethany were both carried to the hospital in critical condition.

Emily paced the tiny walkway of the emergency room as the doctors rushed into the room where Teri was taken. After five minutes, one of the doctors came out to speak with the waiting women.

"There was nothing we could do. I'm sorry, she had lost too much blood," the young man said as though announcing the loss of a football game. With that, he entered the room where Bethany struggled for life.

Emily collapsed on the floor and wept as Ashley held her. "It's gone," she muttered. "It's all gone, now. Damn you, Ashley, if you hadn't called her, she would still be alive now in our apartment in Portland." She slapped Ashley across the face. Tears blinded her eyes as she rose and ran past Catherine and Patricia.

With her hands reaching out, Bethany died. The wounds that she had sustained in the fight had not been serious enough to kill her, and the doctor worked frantically to bring her back. After ten minutes, they called it quits and pronounced her dead.

Danielle and Amanda left the hospital in each other's arms as they both mourned their losses. They drove up to Bethany's cabin and sat on the porch until the sun came up over the mountains. They talked about nothing important as they held and comforted each other.

Patricia, Catherine, and Ashley went back to the school to pack their suitcases. By the time that they arrived, they found all of Emily's things packed and gone.

Patricia brewed a pot of coffee and they sat in the kitchen talking. At first they talked about simple things, and then they talked about Teri. They wept and raged and wept again at the loss of their friend. By the time the night was over, they swore that they would never go on another mission no matter who it was or who needed their help. The cost had been too great this time.

Emily drove through the night. She raged at God, she raged at herself, she raged at Ashley, and she raged at Teri. At times the tears blinded her eyes so bad that she could not see the road, but she never slowed her car. She rushed on through the night as if speed could somehow escape the dawn that loomed over her shoulder. When that time came, she would have to feel the pain that tore her heart. She just wasn't ready to let Teri go. *Not yet,* she told herself, *maybe not ever.*

SIXTEEN

By the following morning, all signs of carnage were mysteriously gone. Ashley stood in the early morning light and looked at the mouth of the mine. Her heart filled with pain as she thought about how much was lost and how little there was to show for it.

When Danielle and Amanda drove up, they found her sitting on the rock in front of the mine. She looked forlorn and lost, like a child who had misplaced something more valuable than anything that could ever be replaced.

Danielle sat next to her on the rock and put her arm around Ashley. Ashley wept. She had no words to say. Danielle held her until the pain drained from her shaking body. She smiled weakly. "I'm sorry about your friend," she said softly.

Ashley wiped her eyes as Danielle led her into the house where Amanda had found the other women sitting over cold coffee cups in the main dining room.

Danielle put a few books on the table in front of her before she spoke. "My sister's name was Judith. She was the one who killed your friend last night. My grandmother knew about her for some time, but she didn't want to acknowledge what she was doing.

"My sister ran away from home years ago when we were both teenagers, and none of us ever heard from her. Anyway, she's dead now." A look of pain shot across Danielle's features as she spoke. "She won't hurt anyone again," she said with finality.

Danielle ran her hands across a large tome that sat on the table. Her eyes rose to meet the gaze of the women. She lifted the book into her hands and handed it carefully to Patricia. "Bethany wanted you to have this. She wrote me a note and left it on the table last night. It said that you would appreciate this book more than anyone she knew."

Patricia looked with disbelief at the old volume. "This was her Book of Shadows. I can't accept this," she breathed as her hand ran lovingly across the cover.

Danielle smiled, "Believe me, I don't want it. And

she left this for Catherine. She said that you would be the only one who could appreciate it as much as she did." Danielle handed a small, worn book to Catherine.

She opened the book carefully. The pages were yellowed and fragile. Carefully, Catherine closed the book and read the title. *"Malleus Maleficarum,"* she breathed in. "Do you know how old this piece of work is? My God, where in the world did she ever get this?" Catherine asked.

Danielle shrugged, "She got it from her mother, who got it from her mother, and so on."

"What is it?" Ashley asked.

"The Witches Hammer. This is one of the original works that came out of the Inquisition. This book was used by the Catholic Church during the witch hunts that occurred hundreds of years ago," Catherine said as she touched the cover gingerly.

"For you, Ashley, Grandmother left this," Danielle said, digging into her pocket. She pulled out a ruby-colored crystal. "She said that it would help you in all your journeys down the road. She told me to tell you to have faith and that one day all the doors to all the mysteries would be opened to you."

Ashley took the gift in her hands and stared into it. She saw Bethany fleetingly within the deep, rich colors of the stone. She looked peaceful and young. Ashley realized it was Bethany's heart stone that she wore around her neck.

"And this is for Emily when you see her again," Danielle said as she pulled out a legal envelope from her pocket. The envelope was sealed. Emily's name was scrawled on the front in small letters. Danielle smiled, "There is a letter in there and the deed to my grandmother's cabin and land."

The women pulled out of the driveway in Patricia's car. With one last look at the mine and the schoolhouse, Ashley drove silently out onto the dirt road. She thought about Emily and wondered about Bethany's gift to her friend. She wondered if Emily would ever want to come back again.

The day of Teri's funeral the ran fell in a dark and chilly drizzle. Emily stood like a statue at the graveside dressed in black with a wide-brimmed hat and a veil to cover her face. Ashley could see no tears.

After the services, Emily approached Catherine with Teri's daughter. The child was clinging to Emily's hand. "I'm going to Montana to my aunt's farm for a while with Gretchen. I left a number where you can reach me if you need to. I just need some time to sort things out."

Catherine smiled and hugged her friend warmly. She had hoped that Emily would have seen though her grief enough to realize that Ashley was not at fault for the death of Teri. So far, Emily had been very cold to her old friend.

Emily walked by Ashley with a slight glance and nothing else. Ashley's heart ached. She wished she could somehow command life back into Teri and make her live again. She stared at the casket in the ground before she dropped in a single white rose.

Two months after Emily left, Catherine found a letter waiting for her one evening when she arrived home. The letter was from Emily. Catherine ripped open the envelope and read the short letter over her cup of coffee.

When Ashley came through the door, she found Catherine frantically packing two suitcases in the bedroom. "What's going on?" Ashley asked as she looked over the baggage. "Was it something I said?"

Catherine looked flushed. "Thank God you're home. I already called your mother, and she's on her way over. We have to go to someplace called Birch Creek near Libby Montana. Emily is in some sort of trouble."

"Hang on, what kind of trouble?" Ashley asked as she watched Catherine pack the last of their clothes.

Catherine shook her head. "I'm not sure, but the letter she wrote is from the city jail."

A few of the publications of
THE NAIAD PRESS, INC.
P.O. Box 10543 • Tallahassee, Florida 32302
Phone (904) 539-5965
Toll-Free Order Number: 1-800-533-1973
Mail orders welcome. Please include 15% postage.

FIRST IMPRESSIONS by Kate Calloway. 208 pp. P.I. Cassidy
James' first case.   ISBN 1-56280-133-3 $10.95

OUT OF THE NIGHT by Chris Bruyer. 192 pp. Spine-tingling
thriller.   ISBN 1-56280-120-1   10.95

NORTHERN BLUE by Tracey Richardson. 224 pp. Police recruits
Miki & Miranda — passion in the line of fire. ISBN 1-56280-118-X   10.95

LOVE'S HARVEST by Peggy Herring. 176 pp. by the author of
Once More With Feeling.   ISBN 1-56280-117-1   10.95

THE COLOR OF WINTER by Lisa Shapiro. 208 pp. Romantic
love beyond your wildest dreams.   ISBN 1-56280-116-3   10.95

FAMILY SECRETS by Laura DeHart Young. 208 pp. Enthralling
romance and suspense.   ISBN 1-56280-119-8   10.95

INLAND PASSAGE by Jane Rule. 288 pp. Tales exploring conven-
tional & unconventional relationships.   ISBN 0-930044-56-8   10.95

DOUBLE BLUFF by Claire McNab. 208 pp. 7th Detective Carol
Ashton Mystery.   ISBN 1-56280-096-5   10.95

BAR GIRLS by Lauran Hoffman. 176 pp. See the movie, read
the book!   ISBN 1-56280-115-5   10.95

THE FIRST TIME EVER edited by Barbara Grier & Christine
Cassidy. 272 pp. Love stories by Naiad Press authors.
                                              ISBN 1-56280-086-8   14.95

MISS PETTIBONE AND MISS McGRAW by Brenda Weathers.
208 pp. A charming ghostly love story.   ISBN 1-56280-151-1   10.95

CHANGES by Jackie Calhoun. 208 pp. Involved romance and
relationships.   ISBN 1-56280-083-3   10.95

FAIR PLAY by Rose Beecham. 256 pp. 3rd Amanda Valentine
Mystery.   ISBN 1-56280-081-7   10.95

PAXTON COURT by Diane Salvatore. 256 pp. Erotic and wickedly
funny contemporary tale about the business of learning to live
together.   ISBN 1-56280-109-0   21.95

PAYBACK by Celia Cohen. 176 pp. A gripping thriller of romance,
revenge and betrayal.   ISBN 1-56280-084-1   10.95

THE MYSTERIOUS NAIAD edited by Katherine V. Forrest & Barbara Grier. 320 pp. Love stories by Naiad Press authors.
ISBN 1-56280-074-4   14.95

DAUGHTERS OF A CORAL DAWN by Katherine V. Forrest. 240 pp. Tenth Anniversay Edition.   ISBN 1-56280-104-X   10.95

BODY GUARD by Claire McNab. 208 pp. 6th Carol Ashton Mystery.   ISBN 1-56280-073-6   10.95

CACTUS LOVE by Lee Lynch. 192 pp. Stories by the beloved storyteller.   ISBN 1-56280-071-X   9.95

SECOND GUESS by Rose Beecham. 216 pp. 2nd Amanda Valentine Mystery.   ISBN 1-56280-069-8   9.95

THE SURE THING by Melissa Hartman. 208 pp. L.A. earthquake romance.   ISBN 1-56280-078-7   9.95

A RAGE OF MAIDENS by Lauren Wright Douglas. 240 pp. 6th Caitlin Reece Mystery.   ISBN 1-56280-068-X   10.95

TRIPLE EXPOSURE by Jackie Calhoun. 224 pp. Romantic drama involving many characters.   ISBN 1-56280-067-1   9.95

UP, UP AND AWAY by Catherine Ennis. 192 pp. Delightful romance.   ISBN 1-56280-065-5   9.95

PERSONAL ADS by Robbi Sommers. 176 pp. Sizzling short stories.   ISBN 1-56280-059-0   9.95

FLASHPOINT by Katherine V. Forrest. 256 pp. Lesbian blockbuster!   ISBN 1-56280-043-4   22.95

CROSSWORDS by Penny Sumner. 256 pp. 2nd Victoria Cross Mystery.   ISBN 1-56280-064-7   9.95

SWEET CHERRY WINE by Carol Schmidt. 224 pp. A novel of suspense.   ISBN 1-56280-063-9   9.95

CERTAIN SMILES by Dorothy Tell. 160 pp. Erotic short stories.
ISBN 1-56280-066-3   9.95

EDITED OUT by Lisa Haddock. 224 pp. 1st Carmen Ramirez Mystery.   ISBN 1-56280-077-9   9.95

WEDNESDAY NIGHTS by Camarin Grae. 288 pp. Sexy adventure.   ISBN 1-56280-060-4   10.95

SMOKEY O by Celia Cohen. 176 pp. Relationships on the playing field.   ISBN 1-56280-057-4   9.95

KATHLEEN O'DONALD by Penny Hayes. 256 pp. Rose and Kathleen find each other and employment in 1909 NYC.
ISBN 1-56280-070-1   9.95

STAYING HOME by Elisabeth Nonas. 256 pp. Molly and Alix want a baby . . . or do they?   ISBN 1-56280-076-0   10.95

TRUE LOVE by Jennifer Fulton. 240 pp. Six lesbians searching for love in all the "right" places.   ISBN 1-56280-035-3   10.95

GARDENIAS WHERE THERE ARE NONE by Molleen Zanger.
176 pp. Why is Melanie inextricably drawn to the old house?
ISBN 1-56280-056-6   9.95

KEEPING SECRETS by Penny Mickelbury. 208 pp. 1st Gianna
Maglione Mystery.   ISBN 1-56280-052-3   9.95

THE ROMANTIC NAIAD edited by Katherine V. Forrest &
Barbara Grier. 336 pp. Love stories by Naiad Press authors.
ISBN 1-56280-054-X   14.95

UNDER MY SKIN by Jaye Maiman. 336 pp. 3rd Robin Miller
Mystery.   ISBN 1-56280-049-3.   10.95

STAY TOONED by Rhonda Dicksion. 144 pp. Cartoons — 1st
collection since *Lesbian Survival Manual.*   ISBN 1-56280-045-0   9.95

CAR POOL by Karin Kallmaker. 272pp. Lesbians on wheels
and then some!   ISBN 1-56280-048-5   10.95

NOT TELLING MOTHER: STORIES FROM A LIFE by Diane
Salvatore. 176 pp. Her 3rd novel.   ISBN 1-56280-044-2   9.95

GOBLIN MARKET by Lauren Wright Douglas. 240pp. 5th Caitlin
Reece Mystery.   ISBN 1-56280-047-7   10.95

LONG GOODBYES by Nikki Baker. 256 pp. 3rd Virginia Kelly
Mystery.   ISBN 1-56280-042-6   9.95

FRIENDS AND LOVERS by Jackie Calhoun. 224 pp. Mid-
western Lesbian lives and loves.   ISBN 1-56280-041-8   10.95

THE CAT CAME BACK by Hilary Mullins. 208 pp. Highly
praised Lesbian novel.   ISBN 1-56280-040-X   9.95

BEHIND CLOSED DOORS by Robbi Sommers. 192 pp. Hot,
erotic short stories.   ISBN 1-56280-039-6   9.95

CLAIRE OF THE MOON by Nicole Conn. 192 pp. See the
movie — read the book!   ISBN 1-56280-038-8   10.95

SILENT HEART by Claire McNab. 192 pp. Exotic Lesbian
romance.   ISBN 1-56280-036-1   10.95

HAPPY ENDINGS by Kate Brandt. 272 pp. Intimate conversations
with Lesbian authors.   ISBN 1-56280-050-7   10.95

THE SPY IN QUESTION by Amanda Kyle Williams. 256 pp.
4th Madison McGuire Mystery.   ISBN 1-56280-037-X   9.95

SAVING GRACE by Jennifer Fulton. 240 pp. Adventure and
romantic entanglement.   ISBN 1-56280-051-5   9.95

THE YEAR SEVEN by Molleen Zanger. 208 pp. Women surviving
in a new world.   ISBN 1-56280-034-5   9.95

CURIOUS WINE by Katherine V. Forrest. 176 pp. Tenth Anniver-
sary Edition. The most popular contemporary Lesbian love story.
ISBN 1-56280-053-1   10.95
Audio Book (2 cassettes)   ISBN 1-56280-105-8   16.95

CHAUTAUQUA by Catherine Ennis. 192 pp. Exciting, romantic
adventure.   ISBN 1-56280-032-9   9.95

A PROPER BURIAL by Pat Welch. 192 pp. 3rd Helen Black
Mystery.   ISBN 1-56280-033-7   9.95

SILVERLAKE HEAT: A Novel of Suspense by Carol Schmidt.
240 pp. Rhonda is as hot as Laney's dreams.   ISBN 1-56280-031-0   9.95

LOVE, ZENA BETH by Diane Salvatore. 224 pp. The most talked
about lesbian novel of the nineties!   ISBN 1-56280-030-2   10.95

A DOORYARD FULL OF FLOWERS by Isabel Miller. 160 pp.
Stories incl. 2 sequels to *Patience and Sarah.*   ISBN 1-56280-029-9   9.95

MURDER BY TRADITION by Katherine V. Forrest. 288 pp. 4th
Kate Delafield Mystery.   ISBN 1-56280-002-7   10.95

THE EROTIC NAIAD edited by Katherine V. Forrest & Barbara
Grier. 224 pp. Love stories by Naiad Press authors.
                                    ISBN 1-56280-026-4   14.95

DEAD CERTAIN by Claire McNab. 224 pp. 5th Carol Ashton
Mystery.   ISBN 1-56280-027-2   9.95

CRAZY FOR LOVING by Jaye Maiman. 320 pp. 2nd Robin Miller
Mystery.   ISBN 1-56280-025-6   9.95

STONEHURST by Barbara Johnson. 176 pp. Passionate regency
romance.   ISBN 1-56280-024-8   10.95

INTRODUCING AMANDA VALENTINE by Rose Beecham.
256 pp. 1st Amanda Valentine Mystery.   ISBN 1-56280-021-3   9.95

UNCERTAIN COMPANIONS by Robbi Sommers. 204 pp.
Steamy, erotic novel.   ISBN 1-56280-017-5   9.95

A TIGER'S HEART by Lauren W. Douglas. 240 pp. 4th Caitlin
Reece Mystery.   ISBN 1-56280-018-3   9.95

PAPERBACK ROMANCE by Karin Kallmaker. 256 pp. A
delicious romance.   ISBN 1-56280-019-1   9.95

MORTON RIVER VALLEY by Lee Lynch. 304 pp. Lee Lynch
at her best!   ISBN 1-56280-016-7   9.95

THE LAVENDER HOUSE MURDER by Nikki Baker. 224 pp.
2nd Virginia Kelly Mystery.   ISBN 1-56280-012-4   9.95

PASSION BAY by Jennifer Fulton. 224 pp. Passionate romance,
virgin beaches, tropical skies.   ISBN 1-56280-028-0   10.95

STICKS AND STONES by Jackie Calhoun. 208 pp. Contemporary
lesbian lives and loves.   ISBN 1-56280-020-5   9.95
Audio Book (2 cassettes)   ISBN 1-56280-106-6   16.95

DELIA IRONFOOT by Jeane Harris. 192 pp. Adventure for Delia
and Beth in the Utah mountains.   ISBN 1-56280-014-0   9.95

UNDER THE SOUTHERN CROSS by Claire McNab. 192 pp.
Romantic nights Down Under.   ISBN 1-56280-011-6   9.95

GRASSY FLATS by Penny Hayes. 256 pp. Lesbian romance in
the '30s.   ISBN 1-56280-010-8   9.95

A SINGULAR SPY by Amanda K. Williams. 192 pp. 3rd
Madison McGuire Mystery.   ISBN 1-56280-008-6   8.95

THE END OF APRIL by Penny Sumner. 240 pp. 1st Victoria
Cross Mystery.   ISBN 1-56280-007-8   8.95

HOUSTON TOWN by Deborah Powell. 208 pp. A Hollis
Carpenter Mystery.   ISBN 1-56280-006-X   8.95

KISS AND TELL by Robbi Sommers. 192 pp. Scorching stories
by the author of *Pleasures*.   ISBN 1-56280-005-1   10.95

STILL WATERS by Pat Welch. 208 pp. 2nd Helen Black Mystery.
                                            ISBN 0-941483-97-5   9.95

TO LOVE AGAIN by Evelyn Kennedy. 208 pp. Wildly romantic
love story.   ISBN 0-941483-85-1   9.95

IN THE GAME by Nikki Baker. 192 pp. 1st Virginia Kelly
Mystery.   ISBN 1-56280-004-3   9.95

AVALON by Mary Jane Jones. 256 pp. A Lesbian Arthurian
romance.   ISBN 0-941483-96-7   9.95

STRANDED by Camarin Grae. 320 pp. Entertaining, riveting
adventure.   ISBN 0-941483-99-1   9.95

THE DAUGHTERS OF ARTEMIS by Lauren Wright Douglas.
240 pp. 3rd Caitlin Reece Mystery.   ISBN 0-941483-95-9   9.95

CLEARWATER by Catherine Ennis. 176 pp. Romantic secrets
of a small Louisiana town.   ISBN 0-941483-65-7   8.95

THE HALLELUJAH MURDERS by Dorothy Tell. 176 pp. 2nd
Poppy Dillworth Mystery.   ISBN 0-941483-88-6   8.95

SECOND CHANCE by Jackie Calhoun. 256 pp. Contemporary
Lesbian lives and loves.   ISBN 0-941483-93-2   9.95

BENEDICTION by Diane Salvatore. 272 pp. Striking, contemporary romantic novel.   ISBN 0-941483-90-8   9.95

BLACK IRIS by Jeane Harris. 192 pp. Caroline's hidden past . . .
                                            ISBN 0-941483-68-1   8.95

TOUCHWOOD by Karin Kallmaker. 240 pp. Loving, May/
December romance.   ISBN 0-941483-76-2   9.95

COP OUT by Claire McNab. 208 pp. 4th Carol Ashton Mystery.
                                            ISBN 0-941483-84-3   9.95

THE BEVERLY MALIBU by Katherine V. Forrest. 288 pp. 3rd
Kate Delafield Mystery.   ISBN 0-941483-48-7   10.95

THAT OLD STUDEBAKER by Lee Lynch. 272 pp. Andy's affair
with Regina and her attachment to her beloved car.
                                            ISBN 0-941483-82-7   9.95

PASSION'S LEGACY by Lori Paige. 224 pp. Sarah is swept into
the arms of Augusta Pym in this delightful historical romance.
ISBN 0-941483-81-9   8.95

THE PROVIDENCE FILE by Amanda Kyle Williams. 256 pp.
2nd Madison McGuire Mystery.   ISBN 0-941483-92-4   8.95

I LEFT MY HEART by Jaye Maiman. 320 pp. 1st Robin Miller
Mystery.   ISBN 0-941483-72-X   10.95

THE PRICE OF SALT by Patricia Highsmith (writing as Claire
Morgan). 288 pp. Classic lesbian novel, first issued in 1952 . . .
acknowledged by its author under her own, very famous, name.
ISBN 1-56280-003-5   9.95

SIDE BY SIDE by Isabel Miller. 256 pp. From beloved author of
Patience and Sarah.   ISBN 0-941483-77-0   9.95

STAYING POWER: LONG TERM LESBIAN COUPLES by
Susan E. Johnson. 352 pp. Joys of coupledom. ISBN 0-941-483-75-4   14.95

SLICK by Camarin Grae. 304 pp. Exotic, erotic adventure.
ISBN 0-941483-74-6   9.95

NINTH LIFE by Lauren Wright Douglas. 256 pp. 2nd Caitlin
Reece Mystery.   ISBN 0-941483-50-9   8.95

PLAYERS by Robbi Sommers. 192 pp. Sizzling, erotic novel.
ISBN 0-941483-73-8   9.95

MURDER AT RED ROOK RANCH by Dorothy Tell. 224 pp.
1st Poppy Dillworth Mystery.   ISBN 0-941483-80-0   8.95

LESBIAN SURVIVAL MANUAL by Rhonda Dicksion. 112 pp.
Cartoons!   ISBN 0-941483-71-1   8.95

A ROOM FULL OF WOMEN by Elisabeth Nonas. 256 pp.
Contemporary Lesbian lives.   ISBN 0-941483-69-X   9.95

THEME FOR DIVERSE INSTRUMENTS by Jane Rule. 208 pp.
Powerful romantic lesbian stories.   ISBN 0-941483-63-0   8.95

CLUB 12 by Amanda Kyle Williams. 288 pp. Espionage thriller
featuring a lesbian agent!   ISBN 0-941483-64-9   8.95

DEATH DOWN UNDER by Claire McNab. 240 pp. 3rd Carol
Ashton Mystery.   ISBN 0-941483-39-8   9.95

MONTANA FEATHERS by Penny Hayes. 256 pp. Vivian and
Elizabeth find love in frontier Montana.   ISBN 0-941483-61-4   8.95

LIFESTYLES by Jackie Calhoun. 224 pp. Contemporary Lesbian
lives and loves.   ISBN 0-941483-57-6   9.95

WILDERNESS TREK by Dorothy Tell. 192 pp. Six women on
vacation learning "new" skills.   ISBN 0-941483-60-6   8.95

MURDER BY THE BOOK by Pat Welch. 256 pp. 1st Helen
Black Mystery.   ISBN 0-941483-59-2   9.95

THERE'S SOMETHING I'VE BEEN MEANING TO TELL YOU
Ed. by Loralee MacPike. 288 pp. Gay men and lesbians coming out
to their children.   ISBN 0-941483-44-4   9.95

LIFTING BELLY by Gertrude Stein. Ed. by Rebecca Mark. 104 pp.
Erotic poetry.   ISBN 0-941483-51-7   10.95

AFTER THE FIRE by Jane Rule. 256 pp. Warm, human novel by
this incomparable author.   ISBN 0-941483-45-2   8.95

THREE WOMEN by March Hastings. 232 pp. Golden oldie. A
triangle among wealthy sophisticates.   ISBN 0-941483-43-6   8.95

PLEASURES by Robbi Sommers. 204 pp. Unprecedented
eroticism.   ISBN 0-941483-49-5   8.95

EDGEWISE by Camarin Grae. 372 pp. Spellbinding
adventure.   ISBN 0-941483-19-3   9.95

FATAL REUNION by Claire McNab. 224 pp. 2nd Carol Ashton
Mystery.   ISBN 0-941483-40-1   10.95

IN EVERY PORT by Karin Kallmaker. 228 pp. Jessica's sexy,
adventuresome travels.   ISBN 0-941483-37-7   9.95

OF LOVE AND GLORY by Evelyn Kennedy. 192 pp. Exciting
WWII romance.   ISBN 0-941483-32-0   10.95

CLICKING STONES by Nancy Tyler Glenn. 288 pp. Love
transcending time.   ISBN 0-941483-31-2   9.95

SOUTH OF THE LINE by Catherine Ennis. 216 pp. Civil War
adventure.   ISBN 0-941483-29-0   8.95

WOMAN PLUS WOMAN by Dolores Klaich. 300 pp. Supurb
Lesbian overview.   ISBN 0-941483-28-2   9.95

THE FINER GRAIN by Denise Ohio. 216 pp. Brilliant young
college lesbian novel.   ISBN 0-941483-11-8   8.95

OCTOBER OBSESSION by Meredith More. Josie's rich, secret
Lesbian life.   ISBN 0-941483-18-5   8.95

BEFORE STONEWALL: THE MAKING OF A GAY AND
LESBIAN COMMUNITY by Andrea Weiss & Greta Schiller.
96 pp., 25 illus.   ISBN 0-941483-20-7   7.95

OSTEN'S BAY by Zenobia N. Vole. 204 pp. Sizzling adventure
romance set on Bonaire.   ISBN 0-941483-15-0   8.95

LESSONS IN MURDER by Claire McNab. 216 pp. 1st Carol Ashton
Mystery.   ISBN 0-941483-14-2   9.95

YELLOWTHROAT by Penny Hayes. 240 pp. Margarita, bandit,
kidnaps Julia.   ISBN 0-941483-10-X   8.95

SAPPHISTRY: THE BOOK OF LESBIAN SEXUALITY by
Pat Califia. 3d edition, revised. 208 pp.   ISBN 0-941483-24-X   10.95

CHERISHED LOVE by Evelyn Kennedy. 192 pp. Erotic Lesbian
love story.   ISBN 0-941483-08-8   10.95

THE SECRET IN THE BIRD by Camarin Grae. 312 pp. Striking,
psychological suspense novel. ISBN 0-941483-05-3   8.95

TO THE LIGHTNING by Catherine Ennis. 208 pp. Romantic
Lesbian 'Robinson Crusoe' adventure. ISBN 0-941483-06-1   8.95

DREAMS AND SWORDS by Katherine V. Forrest. 192 pp.
Romantic, erotic, imaginative stories. ISBN 0-941483-03-7   8.95

MEMORY BOARD by Jane Rule. 336 pp. Memorable novel
about an aging Lesbian couple. ISBN 0-941483-02-9   10.95

THE ALWAYS ANONYMOUS BEAST by Lauren Wright Douglas.
224 pp. 1st Caitlin Reece Mystery.
ISBN 0-941483-04-5   8.95

THE BLACK AND WHITE OF IT by Ann Allen Shockley.
144 pp. Short stories. ISBN 0-930044-96-7   7.95

SAY JESUS AND COME TO ME by Ann Allen Shockley. 288
pp. Contemporary romance. ISBN 0-930044-98-3   8.95

MURDER AT THE NIGHTWOOD BAR by Katherine V. Forrest.
240 pp. 2nd Kate Delafield Mystery. ISBN 0-930044-92-4   10.95

WINGED DANCER by Camarin Grae. 228 pp. Erotic Lesbian
adventure story. ISBN 0-930044-88-6   8.95

PAZ by Camarin Grae. 336 pp. Romantic Lesbian adventurer
with the power to change the world. ISBN 0-930044-89-4   8.95

SOUL SNATCHER by Camarin Grae. 224 pp. A puzzle, an
adventure, a mystery — Lesbian romance. ISBN 0-930044-90-8   8.95

THE LOVE OF GOOD WOMEN by Isabel Miller. 224 pp.
Long-awaited new novel by the author of the beloved *Patience
and Sarah*. ISBN 0-930044-81-9   8.95

THE HOUSE AT PELHAM FALLS by Brenda Weathers. 240
pp. Suspenseful Lesbian ghost story. ISBN 0-930044-79-7   7.95

HOME IN YOUR HANDS by Lee Lynch. 240 pp. More stories
from the author of *Old Dyke Tales*. ISBN 0-930044-80-0   7.95

PEMBROKE PARK by Michelle Martin. 256 pp. Derring-do
and daring romance in Regency England. ISBN 0-930044-77-0   7.95

THE LONG TRAIL by Penny Hayes. 248 pp. Vivid adventures
of two women in love in the old west. ISBN 0-930044-76-2   8.95

AN EMERGENCE OF GREEN by Katherine V. Forrest. 288
pp. Powerful novel of sexual discovery. ISBN 0-930044-69-X   10.95

THE LESBIAN PERIODICALS INDEX edited by Claire Potter.
432 pp. Author & subject index. ISBN 0-930044-74-6   12.95

DESERT OF THE HEART by Jane Rule. 224 pp. A classic;
basis for the movie *Desert Hearts*. ISBN 0-930044-73-8   10.95

TORCHLIGHT TO VALHALLA by Gale Wilhelm. 128 pp.
Classic novel by a great Lesbian writer. ISBN 0-930044-68-1   7.95

LESBIAN NUNS: BREAKING SILENCE edited by Rosemary
Curb and Nancy Manahan. 432 pp. Unprecedented autobiographies
of religious life.   ISBN 0-930044-62-2   9.95

THE SWASHBUCKLER by Lee Lynch. 288 pp. Colorful novel
set in Greenwich Village in the sixties.   ISBN 0-930044-66-5   8.95

SEX VARIANT WOMEN IN LITERATURE by Jeannette
Howard Foster. 448 pp. Literary history.   ISBN 0-930044-65-7   8.95

A HOT-EYED MODERATE by Jane Rule. 252 pp. Hard-hitting
essays on gay life; writing; art.   ISBN 0-930044-57-6   7.95

AMATEUR CITY by Katherine V. Forrest. 224 pp. 1st Kate
Delafield Mystery.   ISBN 0-930044-55-X   10.95

THE SOPHIE HOROWITZ STORY by Sarah Schulman. 176 pp.
Engaging novel of madcap intrigue.   ISBN 0-930044-54-1   7.95

THE YOUNG IN ONE ANOTHER'S ARMS by Jane Rule.
224 pp. Classic Jane Rule.   ISBN 0-930044-53-3   9.95

OLD DYKE TALES by Lee Lynch. 224 pp. Extraordinary stories
of our diverse Lesbian lives.   ISBN 0-930044-51-7   8.95

AGAINST THE SEASON by Jane Rule. 224 pp. Luminous,
complex novel of interrelationships.   ISBN 0-930044-48-7   8.95

LOVERS IN THE PRESENT AFTERNOON by Kathleen Fleming.
288 pp. A novel about recovery and growth.   ISBN 0-930044-46-0   8.95

TOOTHPICK HOUSE by Lee Lynch. 264 pp. Love between two
Lesbians of different classes.   ISBN 0-930044-45-2   7.95

CONTRACT WITH THE WORLD by Jane Rule. 340 pp. Power-
ful, panoramic novel of gay life.   ISBN 0-930044-28-2   9.95

THIS IS NOT FOR YOU by Jane Rule. 284 pp. A letter to a
beloved is also an intricate novel.   ISBN 0-930044-25-8   8.95

OUTLANDER by Jane Rule. 207 pp. Short stories and essays by
one of our finest writers.   ISBN 0-930044-17-7   8.95

ODD GIRL OUT by Ann Bannon.   ISBN 0-930044-83-5   5.95
I AM A WOMAN 84-3; WOMEN IN THE SHADOWS 85-1;   each
JOURNEY TO A WOMAN 86-X; BEEBO BRINKER 87-8. Golden
oldies about life in Greenwich Village.

JOURNEY TO FULFILLMENT, A WORLD WITHOUT MEN, and   3.95
RETURN TO LESBOS. All by Valerie Taylor   each

These are just a few of the many Naiad Press titles — we are the oldest and
largest lesbian/feminist publishing company in the world. Please request a
complete catalog. We offer personal service; we encourage and welcome
direct mail orders from individuals who have limited access to bookstores
carrying our publications.